YACHT ROMANCE

The Awakening of Love

By Arden Janessa Cole

Discover the EPILOGUE – The Proposal

Click the link or use the QR code below

https://bit.ly/3hgMIwV

Index

Thanks again for choosing this book. It is my first book and I'd really love to hear your thoughts.

Make sure to leave a short review on Amazon if you enjoy it.

https://www.amazon.com/review/create-review

Chapter 1 – Jeffery and Alice

'Jeffery!'

Alice yelled out as she stomped down the stairs with a furious look on her face.

'What is it?' Jeffery shot back.

'Why's there a coffee stain on my shirt?'

'Uh…' Jeffery was about to respond.

'You spilled coffee on my shirt?!' Alice interrupted him.

'Stop yelling and let me talk'.

'I should stop yelling? I should stop? You want to talk? Here you are, with a cup of coffee in your hands and you say you want to talk? What do you want to say? That you didn't spill coffee on my shirt?' Alice retorted.

'I didn't spill coffee on your shirt...' Jeffery interjected. '...intentionally' he continued.

'So, what did you do, unintentionally?'

'Would you even let me make a complete sentence?' He barked.

'Humph!' She was so angry she could punch him, instead she stomped back to her room with so many thoughts running through her head. These back and forth fights have been going on between them longer than she could remember.

Alice is a 29-year-old tall woman, 5'8 tall with emerald green eyes, she has very intimidating curves that makes men swoon and ladies envious. Her red auburn hair is something that turns heads every time she walks by. Her passion for success and independence is what makes her downright sexy, this she knew not only by comments from her husband, but from other men around her which is an irony to her because to the best of her knowledge, most men always scurry away from women like her. She has a way of lightening up a place just with her smile which was one of the reasons her husband was attracted to her.

Unfortunately, she seems to have currently lost that ability as she feels there is no more happiness inside of her to bring up light anywhere.

She owns a very big makeup studio that is known all over the city of New York. She has been working on it right before she got married to her husband, Jeffery Myron, and currently she is going to work pissed just because her Dear husband spilled coffee on her neatly ironed white t-shirt she placed on the bed just before she went to the bathroom to have a shower.

Shuffling through her wardrobe she pulled out another matching blouse to go with her cream-colored pants and black heels. All the while thinking if her marriage was really going anyway, because with the way things were going, they may eventually have to get a divorce and go their separate ways. They have been married for just six years and it already feels like a lifetime. The constant bickering, arguments and, fights was getting to her, she couldn't even concentrate on work. The stress and unhappiness are already showing on her physically. She doesn't know how much she can take anymore. The sound of her cell phone going off interrupted her thoughts, checking the ID of the caller, she saw it was her mother. She picked immediately, desperate to let out her thoughts and at least have a clearer head for the day's work.

'Mum', she breathed out.

'Honey, why do you sound like you just got your eggs burnt? Did you guys have an argument again?' She sighed

'Mum, I am tired. How much more can I take? He finds a way to frustrate me every damn time! Now I am late for work because he had to spill coffee on my shirt, he didn't even let me know and the time I was supposed to use to drive down to work, we spent it arguing. Mum he didn't even apologize!' She cried.

'It's not like you would let him say anything. The two of you are always throwing tantrums like children. For God's sake Al, didn't you learn a thing from I and your father? We are still together happily married and my beloved daughter is struggling barely six years in marriage! My God! You children are giving me migraine already' She sighed with her fingertips on her temples, trying to get a relief by pressing into them.

'Mum you are really not helping matters. Look I need to move my ass to work, I guess I would just give you a call later. Kiss Dad for me and take something for your migraine. I love you.'

'Wait! I have something for you. I know you might not accept it right away, but promise me you would think about it, okay?' Alice…' mum pleaded.

Alice sighed, putting on her heels, she grabbed her purse and work bags with her other free hand.' Okay Mum, I promise, what is it? I am really late. I know I'm the boss, but that doesn't excuse me from coming late to work. Mum, shoot!'

'Okay baby, so I came across a magazine and I saw an advert of an executive cruise on Atlantis yacht heading to Palawan Islands in Philippines…'

'What does that have to do with me, Mum?' She interrupted, running out of patience

'Let me land child!'

'Okay, okay, I am sorry' Alice breathed out

'So, when I saw it, I thought about you and Jeffery and I thought it would be a good opportunity for the both of you to get yourselves on that yacht and settle your differences, Just the both of you. Honestly, I think you guys just need time together without interference from any of us. Meet new people, see new things. Baby just the two of you, no work, and no family, just enjoy yourselves together for about 2 months or so. What do you think?' She rambled

'What?' She shouted with her eyes widened. 'Mum how can you say we should stay together and enjoy ourselves? Without work?! Work is the only thing that keeps me sane right now. I can't afford to leave work and stay what? 2 months with that frustrating man? Mum this cannot work' she said with finality at the tip of her tongue.

'Alice' Mum sighed.

'Listen child, you already promised you would think about this and besides I and your father have been to Palawan Islands long before you were born, and I have also heard of different stories of Atlantis yacht, and that place have a way of lightening a spark between two love birds. Trust me baby it's worth the trial. I know you have had series of discussions to make your marriage better, but why don't you try a change of environment?'

'We are not two love birds' Alice mumbled, 'You know what Mum, I will think about it but I don't know if this will work out, besides you have to tell him yourself, I am running late and I have to go now. Bye mum'

Rolling her eyes, 'Okay honey, I trust you to make the right decision, I know you haven't had breakfast, make sure you have a stop by at that your favorite coffee shop and grab something. Al, the trip is in 3 days, make up your mind, I would speak to Jeffery and I am sure he would be glad to do this. Bye baby, I love you.'

'Whatever Mum, Love you.' Alice rolled her eyes with a smirk on her face, she loves her mum but she feels the woman has gone overboard this time, this trip would not change anything but then she can only try, right?

She rushed downstairs to find an empty sitting room. Jeff has gone, he didn't even tell her he was leaving. That man! Alice sighed, walked outside, made sure the door was securely locked, entered into her car and drove off to her popular makeup studio in the city.

'What the hell is wrong with you?!' Jeffery backed at the driver that just drove pass him. He was frustrated. He left the house fuming so hard. 'Can't we just have a morning without fights?! Can't we be like every other couple out there?! Every minute of the day we are at each other's neck, humph!' He shouted out in frustration.

He couldn't believe she wouldn't even let him explain himself.

After dressing for work this morning, he went downstairs to make himself a cup of coffee. While he was beside the kitchen cabinet, he heard his phone ring. In a rush to get the phone, he ran upstairs with the cup of coffee, stretching out his hand to get the phone from the night stand, some of the liquid from the cup spilled on the bed.

With the bid to quickly get to the phone, he didn't notice what his action had caused. He checked the ID of the caller and immediately picked the call seeing that it was his partner that needed his attention.

If only he knew that he spilled coffee on his wife's shirt, he would have at least let her know and pick out another shirt, but he didn't and the damn woman came down spiting fire without listening to a damn thing from him.

'Fuck!' He exclaimed as he repeatedly blasted his horns at the vehicle in front of his 2019 BMW 8 series. The driver was not making his situation any better, 'Why won't he just drive like a normal person?!' He exclaimed.

Jeffery Myron is a tall slender man with blue striking eyes, his jet-black hair always tempting to run your hands through. He is a very successful Lawyer in New York City and has a way of getting the ladies with the sparkle in his eyes but ever since he got married to Alice, he had only eyes for her. He was 27 years when he got married to his beautiful wife, he had always known Alice was the one for him but after 3 years, he wasn't so sure. They constantly fought and it was already affecting him at work, he has tried several times to sit her down and talk about their issue but they can't seem to point out anything which makes the matter worse.

He knew something was wrong, he doesn't know what and how

to solve it but he must get to the root of this, he can't afford to lose Al, she is the love of his life. He stopped at the building of his tall firm

'Al, we can do this, we have to!' He sighed while rubbing his smooth palm over his face. That reassurance was enough to get him through the day's work.

Chapter 2 – Palawan Islands

'Turn right with your chin raised up', Click, click.

'Look at me, now strike a pose', Click, click, click

'No, no, no, just relax and feel the picture', Click!

'Hugh! Clara what's wrong?!' Alex lamented. He is one of the best Photographer in Moscow, not just good but very attractive, he has every girl batting their lashes at him. Right now, he wasn't pleased with Clara. Ever since she walked into the studio, something has been off about her. He thought it would eventually wear off as it does whenever they start the studio session but obviously, he was wrong.

She just stared at him, which made it more annoying. Clapping his hands, 'Okay, okay, let's get a break', He shouted while grabbing a bottle of water from the welfare team and working out of the studio to clear his head.

Clara sighed, grabbed a bottle of water and slumped on a blue soft sofa in the studio. She knew she didn't come out today with her A game and she feels guilty for putting Alex through her own problems but then it isn't entirely her fault, she just wishes everyone will give her a breathing space.

 She is beautiful and she knows it but the fact that everyone sees it as an opportunity to make money off her or get pleasure from her, irritates her, even her own mother. Thinking through everything that has been happening with her over the years, she decides she needs a break.

Clara Davis is a 6'0 striking blond with light blue eyes, eyes that carried a lot of mystery and can pierce through anyone. She is photogenic and has a smooth rose-tinged ivory skin with long legs that makes a man drool. Her mouth is perfectly curved with a beautiful shaped nose and jaw line. She walks with a certain grace that leaves you no choice than to admire, her physic is something that makes her a successful model. Clara carries a guard around her, everyone including her colleagues sees her as cold but she is just that woman that thinks people only come around her because of what they would gain, not because of who she is. Growing up with only her mother- yeah, her father is late- she learnt the hard way, her mother pushed her beyond limits right from a tender age, even though she is grateful and successful, she realized her mother was making her live the dreams she always had but was never given the opportunity to fulfill.

Thinking, she has no choice than to do what everybody wants her to do, which is work, make more money, be the perfect model and perfect daughter, Clara sighed and closed her eyes.

She felt so dissatisfied with her life, 'I can be more than this', she murmured while her eyes were still tightly closed with the back of her head resting on the sofa.

'I can be a successful Model and still be happy', she whispered with conviction, opening her eyes, coming back to reality, she reached out to a magazine laying on a table across her, that has a full picture of her in bikini printed at the front cover. She stood to get it and moved back to the comfortable sofa, stopping to admire herself she flipped through the magazine. For a while, she was lost in the contents of the magazine until something caught her eyes.

'Palawan Islands'! She squealed

She can vividly remember the rattling of some models when she went for a job at Manhattan Beach in New York last weekend and the chattering of the beautiful Atlantis yacht and how they ventured on a trip to Palawan Islands, the gleaming white-sand beaches, the emerald lakes, quaint fishing villages and many more they rattled about Palawan Islands got her intrigued. Now she was seeing an advert for an executive cruise on Atlantis yacht heading to Palawan Islands. Smiling she thought, the world was finally on her side and so there and then she decided she must go for this trip. She needs to go far away from everybody especially her mother to think about what she wants and be happy, even if it's just for what? 3 months! Checking the date for the trip she realized she has just 2 days to prepare herself for the trip.

'I need to go!' She thought out loud to herself.

After 20mins, Alex walked in seeing the smile on Clara's face and wondered what could transform her in a space of 20mins. He thought about asking her even though they were not specifically friends but at least they work together and have comfortable conversations some times.

Before the question could jump out from his mouth, Clara blurted out, 'Uhm, Alex I am sorry, but I would need to go now'

'What? What do you mean, go now? We haven't finished the shoot and I have to submit the job tomorrow. You and I know the strings this company will pull; we can't leave them hanging', he objected.

Clara stood up from the sofa while straightening out the expensive red organza gown with tiny hand straps and a slit from her mid-thigh down to her ankle, the gown looked so perfect on her.

'Alex, you can get another model for the job and you know it, I have to leave and I don't see anything changing my mind right now'. She said, as picked up the magazine from the spot she kept it on the sofa.

'I can't believe this' He huffed with one hand on his waist and the other rubbing down his face. 'Clara you are the only one I trust with this job; no other person can do this job the way I want!' His voice went on a high pitch with his arms raised in the air.

'Alex dear, you can handle this, I trust you. By the way, are you the owner of this?' She asked while stretching out the magazine to him.

'Yeah, why?' He asked

'Can I have it?' She requested

'Sure. But Clara, why do you really need to go now?' He whined.

She picked up her purse and keys, walked up to him and kissed him on his ruby cheeks. 'Thank you, Alex, I am sorry for ruining your day, but I need to do this for myself. I know you can handle it. You are the best photographer in the World! I will mail the dress back to you. Bye, see you when I see you'.

'Bye Clara', He whispered as he watched her walked away. He was blushing really hard; thank God she wasn't looking. Clara is not one to make such gesture or sound so human, maybe she really needed to do whatever she has in that beautiful mind of hers. He knows she has not always been a happy doll, but then maybe whatever she is about to do now would keep those smiles on her face permanently. But damn, his face was still very red, he shook his head and walked back into the studio to talk with his team on how to get another reliable model on set.

Sitting back in her white beautiful sport car given to her by her only uncle on her last birthday- the only family she can be herself with and not try to be anything perfect, - she flipped through the magazine again, went to the page of the advert and read through it all over again, at that moment she was convinced she wanted to go through with this. Clara picked up her phone to call her manager, so she can cancel every appointment she has on her plate for 3 months.

3 seconds later...

'Clara'. Her mother's smooth silk voice was heard at the other end of the line.

Yes, her mother is her manager and she braced herself for any backlash that would be thrown at her during this conversation.

'Hi mother' She responded coldly. They are mostly official with each other even as daughter and mother and that is one of the things Clara wants to change even though she doesn't know how to.

'How are you? Are you done with the shoot?' Her mother asked

'I am good. I am going for a trip, I need you to cancel every appointment I have for the next 2 months', she breathed

'WHAT???' Her mother screamed, causing her to wince and take the phone far from her ears. She shut her eyes, she could do this, even if it means putting her job on the line. All she wants is to be happy, so she is going to take the risk.

After what seems like hours which was just 5 seconds her mother barked, 'what do you mean by I should cancel every appointment you have for the next 2 months?!' She sighed and spoke softly, 'Clara baby, did you hit your head somewhere?'

Clara was taken aback by the soft voice, it almost felt like her mother cared. 'Mother look, I have made up my mind and it is final. As my, manager I just felt I should let you know. My trip is in two days and I would be back before you know it. You don't need to worry about me or something, even though I know you don't care, you are just concerned about the money you will lose. Don't worry when I am back, we would make more. Bye mother, take care of you'. She spoke with an edge. She cleared her voice, she can't break down now, she thought.

Truly her mother was concerned about the money they were about to lose but she loves her daughter too and even though she felt hurt by the way she just spoke to her; she knew it was all her doing. She made her daughter live through her personal dreams, pushing her beyond limits, depriving her of every kind of love a mother should give her daughter all because she wanted her to be strong and successful. Maybe she wasn't supposed to have gone about it this way, now she and her daughter are worlds apart with only business bringing them together. She sighed as these thoughts went through her, now she is almost regretting everything.

Realizing she was still on the phone with Clara, she decided she won't argue with her any more, if it would make her happy, she should go. Maybe she also could use the time to think things through and find a way to get her daughter back, if it is not too late.

Clara was about to cut the call when she heard, 'Okay darling, if it makes you happy, you can go, I would handle things over here. Have a nice trip and take care of yourself'. She was surprised, both by the endearment she heard and the care she sensed in her voice but she was happy too, her mother's consent was still important to her.

'Thank you. Bye mother', she said softly.

'Wait! Are you not going to give me the location or details of the trip?' Her mother asked in a raised tone.

Knowing her Mother, she knew she can't make that kind of mistake or she would find her on that yacht. 'No Mother, Love you'. Ding!

Her mother stared at the phone shocked, by her refusal to tell her where she was going for 2 months. And most especially, did her daughter just tell her she loves her? She was going to have a heart attack from happiness. She sighed, maybe she just did the right thing, and she really cannot wait to get her daughter back.

Clara hand was clasped over her mouth and her eyes were almost bulging out from their socket. 'Did I just say that'? She whispered to herself. Well, she shrugged, she really does love her mother, they've not just being on a love-relationship term, she giggled, partly because she feels lighter than she has felt in years and because she knew she made the right decision to go on this yacht cruise to Palawan Islands.

'Atlantis yacht, here I come!' She screamed in her car with excitement as she drove right to her house to prepare herself for this life changing trip.

'Palawan Islands?' Phillip quizzed.

'Yesss' Sandro stressed. 'You need this Phil' he continued. 'Ever since you and Leticia ended things, you've really not been yourself. You've carried this gloom all over, even your work has lost its exquisite quality'

'What do you mean Sandro? I'm fine! Work is fine, clients are happy' Phillip defended himself, turning from the monitor screen to face Sandro who was standing right behind him after telling him to go on an executive yacht cruise to Palawan Island.

'Are you happy, Phil?' Sandro said with his mouth full of the burger he's been eating. 'Look into my eyes right now and lie to me that deep down inside of you, you're the happiest you can be at this point'

'Well…'

'There's nothing well about you Phil' Sandro cut him short, 'that's why you need this trip. Just so you can get well, and get back to the same old Philip everyone knows'

'Sandro' Phillip started, standing from the chair, holding the flier in his hands, facing Sandro, 'I can't just get up and leave town to someplace I don't know in order to get well, as you say'

'It's magical out there, Phil. Trust me. It is.'

'And you know this, how? You've never been there before, have you?'

'I haven't, but…'

'But nothing bro. For all we know, that place might not even be safe, it might be in the middle of nowhere with no access to civilization'

'You'd be travelling on the Atlantis Phil, the Atlantis yacht. And you know when it comes to cruise, these guys aren't to be toyed with. They're practically the best at what they do. Everybody knows, even you.'

'Would you be coming too?'

'No Phil, I'd be right here, managing your studio till you get back.

Besides, you're the one that needs to get your mojo back, not me. Deal with it, bro, you've lost your inspiration, this trip would do you good'

'Sandro, you keep pushing me to do things…'

'…that are best for you because I'm your best friend and I love you' Sandro interjected, holding Philip's shoulders and looking right into his eyes. 'The trip is tomorrow, let's make a reservation for you immediately'

Phillip felt defeated, he wasn't going to win this battle of wills with his best friend Sandro, who was already making a call, supposedly making a reservation for a trip Phillip wasn't obviously interested in. He was about travelling in his world of thoughts as he has found himself doing in recent times, but was jerked backed to reality by Sandro's hoarse voice.

'It's fully booked' he said with a gloom on his face.

'Oh nice' Phillip replied smiling 'Now I'm hungry, let's go grab something to eat'.

'This isn't something to smile about' Sandro chided as he fetched his hat.

'What?' Phillip burst out laughing. 'I didn't book all the slots, did I? Answer your ringing phone while I hit the gents before we head out' Phillip excused himself to go to the toilet, grinning all the way, as he returned, the reaction he got from Sandro wasn't what he was expecting.

'You're on' Sandro said in a sing-song manner as he did a mini dance while breaking the news to Phillip.

'What? We got a new job?' Phillip asked, confused.

'So, the yacht just called and said a traveler cancelled last minute, and asked if you were willing to take the space' Sandro replied gleefully 'pack your bags boy, you're going to Palawan'.

Chapter 3 – Atlantis Yacht

The Atlantis yacht is one of the most beautiful 67.5-meter super yachts on the Caribbean Sea which is considered as part of North America. She was designed and built in 2007 by one of the best ship naval engineers in the world and was refitted extensively in 2017 to maintain her incredible reputation as a pioneer, that year, she was extended by five meters and had a new pool, spa, gym and sauna added to her.

It is owned by one of the richest business men in Chicago, Jacob Nyren. In 2007 during the building of the yacht, he met Atlantis Pickerson, the woman who stole his heart and he decided to name his beautiful yacht after her. She had a way of lightening up a place and bringing love amongst people, that was one of the things that got him attracted to her, and also a reason he named the yacht after her. He got married to her after 6 months and they have both been managing the yacht till they got a manager in 2019 and decide to face other chain of their businesses.

It is widely known that the Atlantis yacht has a peculiar way of bringing people together, that is why people travel far and wide just to have a trip on her. The interiors are sure to pique your interest, from the cozy bar to the luxurious onboard gym, guest rooms that have open spaces and tall ceilings to the grand spiral staircase that draws each level together, and most exciting is the semi-submerged viewing lounge, providing views both above and below water.

Every summer, the Atlantis yacht embarks on exciting trips from the Caribbean Sea to any Island in the world and this time around she would be heading to Palawan Island in Philippines for a space of 2 months, which promises to be very exhilarating. The crew members are also as excited as the guests that would come on board the yacht as they get to meet rich and famous people, bond with them and most thrilling, get a good amount of tips from them.

Alice slumps in the chair as she throws her keys across the table and peeled off her shoes from her feet, she has had a very hectic day, standing all through due to the amount of clients that trooped in. Normally she wouldn't even have to leave her office and just supervise the studio with the use of the CCTV camera or reports she gets from her manager but a lot of clients today requested for her expertise in particular.

She yawns and sniffs.

'Is that potatoes pie?' She asked as she sniffs the aroma coming right from the kitchen.

It was then she realized Jeff's car was in the park and the door wasn't even locked when she came home.

'Why is he home this early? Is he the one in the kitchen?' She asked with her brows furrowed. Getting up from the chair, she decided to get the answers to her questions.

Jeffery was excited, he got to the office today with a determination to make his marriage work. He couldn't even concentrate at work and during lunch hours, he went to the company's favorite restaurant across the street, after ordering for his usual menu, he relaxed with the drink he ordered before the food would arrive. The sound of his phone going off caught his attention, he picked it up and saw it was his mother-in-law on the line.

He thought to himself with a sour face, 'I don't need another marital talk again'.

Surprisingly after the call, he was smiling like someone who just won a lottery, when the waitress came with his lunch, he kept on smiling at her, with confusion written on her face, she plastered a fake smile and scampered away. Thinking about that scenario, he chuckled to himself.

He carried that smile all through the day's work, deciding to go home early and make dinner before his wife gets back. He wanted to make one of her favorite meal, so he had to leave work early to get some groceries from the store before he heads home. Yeah, he wanted to be romantic and he meant it when he said he would make this marriage work.

Now, he was in the kitchen in a gray sweat shirt and pajamas pants, with his jet-black hair glistening wet and his back to the entrance of the kitchen, whistling and swaying his hips to Haley Reinhart, *Can't Help Falling in love,* playing from the music player, while chopping the vegetables on the kitchen counter.

'What are you doing?' Alice questioned with her arms folded and her body resting on the door of the kitchen, she was surprised and at the same time amused by the sight before her. He was startled by her voice and turned sharply to her. She gasped inwardly once her eyes connected to the fine specimen before her, seeing him like this is doing something to her inner folds, all she wants to do at that moment is to run into his arms, pull off his shirt so she can run her hands through his fine abs and kiss him senseless.

She slightly shook her head, 'What was wrong with her? Yes, it has been very long but she shouldn't be acting like a woman high on hormones', she thought.

He turned at the sound of the voice he has been expecting ever since he walked into the house this evening, maybe too fast and what he saw took his breath away, she was standing at the door with her arms folded, still in her work clothes and her beautiful hair loosely packed up in a bun with small strands falling out at almost every side, her full lips puckered out invitingly with a dull shade of pink and a small smile at the corner of her lips, her eyes tired but slightly squinted at him, not to mention how smugly tight her pant was on her. He has always loved her on pants and he didn't get to see her all dressed up this morning before he left the house. He felt the tightness of his pant below and he had to remember why he was there in the kitchen at that time and not ruin the moment.

When he realized they have been staring at each other for about 15 seconds, he cleared his throat and answered with a grin, 'I am making your favorite meal'.

'What's the occasion?' She asked as she walked into the kitchen with a little frown on her beautiful face and sat on the stool.

'Would you like a drink?' He asked instead.

Still with a frown, she shrugged, 'Okay'.

He went around to the kitchen's cabinet, taking out a bottle of champagne and a glass, poured out the drink and handed her the glass with a hand at his back and a little bow, 'Here you go beauty,' he said with a blinding smile.

She chuckled and accepted the drink, after taking a sip of the wine, she dropped the glass on the counter and faced him all the while he was checking the chicken in the oven.

'Okay, in as much as I am grateful for all these, coming back to a peaceful home after a stressful day to meet my dear husband making one of my favorites for dinner and acting all sexy, this haven't happened in a long while and I am curious. Jeff, what is all these?' She gestured with her hands point out to the entire kitchen

'I am sexy?' He asked with a jaw dropping grin, she was already finding too hard to resist.

'Jeffery', she said with a warning.

'Alright, I get it' he said with his two hands raised up. 'Why don't you go up, take a shower, put on comfortable clothes and hurry right down here. I would be done with all of these before you get down and we would discuss over dinner. Okay?'

She stared at him and saw the determination written on his face. Did he win a case? She decided not to argue and softly replied, 'Okay'.

Gulping down the remaining liquid in the glass, she stood up, went to the sitting room, picked up her belongings and proceeded to her room. She really needs that shower now and she would deal with Jeffery later.

30 minutes later…

Walking down the stairs, she realized how hungry she was. She got to the bottom of the stairs and headed straight up for the dinning. She gave a little gasp causing Jeffery to raise his heads up to behold the beauty of his wife heading to the table with her eyes widened and a smile on her face making him forget everything around them but her.

'Fuck! What was this woman doing to him? How come it has

been so long he saw her this way?' He thought.

Maybe he just hasn't been looking and was more focused on avoiding her and any kind of arguments or fights. He has always been so attracted to her before they got married and after, but these past years, they were so much at each other's neck that they avoided each other all together.

'Hell, when last did they make love?', he wondered as his eyes flew to the nipples protruding from her tank top and her belly button winking at him.

'Jeff, you really did all of these?' She squealed with her mouth slightly hanging open gesturing to the table. Potato pie, chicken nuggets, cheese, sweet onion jam, and warm spinach salad with sauce-griddled prawns, all her favorites on a table. Not to mention her favorite cocktail drink and the candle light illuminating the dining room.

'You should have told me to wear a gown instead, this is too much Jeff', she murmured.

'Nothing is too much for my lovely wife', he said as he pulled out a chair for her to sit. 'Have your sit, mademoiselle', He drawled out in a French accent.

She giggled and sat down feel all giddy, this man definitely has something up his sleeves, she thought. It has been so long they had something close to a good time together and honestly, she is looking forward to this night. Taking a piece of pie into her mouth, she closed her eyes and savored the taste, it tasted heavenly. Her husband has always been a better cook than she was and she can't wait to eat off everything he has made for them.

'You like it?' He asked with a smile as he sat down and watched her with her eyes closed and a beautiful smile on her face. Gosh, she is beautiful.

Her eyes flew open, 'Like it? I love it', She exclaimed with a shrill.

15 minutes into dinner, Jeffery decided it was time to let her know what made him happy almost all day. Wiping his mouth with a napkin, he placed his cutlery down gently and looked at her.

She noticed he was staring, she looked up at him, 'What?' She asked defensively

Chuckling, 'Your mum called earlier today'. He blurted

She knew this was serious and also wondered what that statement has to do with this entire scheme.

'Okay...' she said as she sunk her teeth into the chicken nugget.

'Baby, I know for the past few years, we have not been our best with each other. I mean we don't even know what the problem is, we just keep fighting about unnecessary things. I love you so much Al, I don't want to lose you and we have to make our marriage work…' He breathed, then continued.

'…That is why I have already made reservation at the Atlantis yacht for the trip to Palawan Islands. When your mum called and told me about it, I knew we have to go, we need our spark back baby and I would get it back whether you like it or not'. He blabbed.

'You did what?' Alice boomed as she dropped everything she was eating and relaxed back with a frown on her face. She didn't know if she should be angry with him for making the reservation without getting an opinion from her or be mesmerized by the proclamation of love coming from him.

He sighed and relaxed back on the chair, 'Your Mum said she told you about it and the trip is in 2 days Al, you should clear up your schedule at work and start packing. We are doing this, no going back'.

She was staring at him with a more intense frown. Who does he think he is? Telling her to clear her schedule and pack her things? She isn't going anywhere! Looking at the way they were currently, it is easy to imagine their time together being bearable but thinking of their unbearable fights, she won't go through this. No, I can't. All these thoughts running through her mind until she heard,

'I love you Al'.

Jeff whispering those words was the thing needed to break her defense. She softened, ran her palms through her face and looked up at him through her lashes, 'Fine,' she said reluctantly.

His face split into an ear-splitting grin, 'YES!' he pumped his fist into the air. She couldn't help but laugh out loudly, 'Let's eat all these before it gets cold and move straight to dessert'. She said with a smirk.

He didn't want to read so much meaning into 'dessert', so he just nodded and went back to the meal.

'I love you too, Jeff' she said looking at him.

He raised his head up and gave her warm smile, maybe he really made the right decision this time.

The distance from Chicago to Philippines is about 13075km, which won't take more than a month for a boat to get there depending on the route the captain takes, Atlantis yacht and her crew are famed for stopping at different beaches before they arrive at their main destination.

The night before the trip, they received several reservations from different places in the world. The engine has been surveyed by the boat engineers, the stewardesses are ready and the boat is stocked with all manner of food ingredients and luxury essentials for the trip.

'Jersey, the guests are arriving ashore, can you kindly check them in?' The yacht manager, Camilla Robin said to one of the stewardesses.

'Right away', she responded excitedly.

Jersey is pretty excited. She is a petite blond of 5'7 ft with huge bosom and a portable shape of buttocks, large enough to make a man stare. She can be said to be pretty with her light brown eyes. Her hair stops just directly on her shoulders and her cleavages were almost out, leaving a man little or nothing to wonder about the shade of her ample huge bosom. She always thinks this summer trips are opportunity for her to find her prince charming.

She scurried out to the welcoming room with a smile plastered on her face, gasping out loudly. The man standing in front of her with his luggage sitting closely beside him can give any woman, old or young a heart attack. His huge biceps were clearly showing even though he was wearing a suit. He was very handsome, not that she hasn't seen handsome men, hell, she works on a yacht, but this man was cocky handsome. The most striking thing about him was his eyes, they were gray, one can swim all day in those eyes.

She swooned.

He gave her a cocky smile, and she consciously pushed her cleavage to him, thinking that day was her lucky day, she has found her prince charming and she would do everything possible to get this very fine man in front of her.

'Welcome to Atlantis yacht, my name is Jersey Jackson, you can call me J.J. Do you have a reservation here?' She asked seductively as she smiled and batted her long artificial lashes at him.

Chapter 4 – J. J

He was looking at her with amusement, girls like her, he can't deal with them, he thought as he gave her his most charming smile, 'Nice to meet you J.J. Yes, I do have a reservation under the name, Derrick Peyton'.

'Oh, are you Derrick Peyton?!' She screeched.

'Yes ma'am,' he replied while nodding his head.

Her eyes were almost bugging out of their socket and her lips were far apart from each other. 'You are Derrick Peyton?! Like the son of Gibson D. Peyton???!' She screamed.

He winced at her loud sounds and nodded to her question, all the while smiling. He is used to this kind of reaction every time he steps into a new place. His father is the owner of Peyton Group, one of biggest and very famous automobile distributors in the whole of Europe. And he is supposedly the next CEO to take up the business but he's having a hard time with that. He doesn't want to handle the family business, hell, he doesn't even know what to do with the business, all he wants to do is to enjoy the money, the women and the recognition that comes with it.

'Wow!' Jersey was in awe of this man, not only did she think she was lucky to meet this very fine dude, she just realized she was talking to money itself.

'This is her man, she is going to put her damn mark on him', she thought with a mischievous smile as she checked for his name in the system and acknowledged his arrival.

He saw the smile; he knew what she was thinking and he gave her a smile of his own. He knows this game and he was ready to play it. She isn't looking bad either, he thought as he looked at her in a quick motion from head to toe, his eyes lingering on her breasts. Knowing the things, he was capable of doing, he shook his head slightly with a smirk displayed on his face.

'Can you show me the way, baby doll?' He drawled seductively.

She could feel the wetness of her folds already, she was definitely going to fuck this man.

'Oh yes, follow me sir', she purred, pushing her buttocks back and her chest forward. She wasn't supposed to leave her duty post, just in case another guest comes in, but then she is willingly to take any chance at all just to be with this man. She turned her back to him and swayed her hips effortlessly as she walked him to meet another stewardess that would show him his cabin for his stay on the yacht.

'Hello sir, I am Avery Miller, it is a pleasure to have you here'. She smiled as she stretched out the yacht's brochure to him.

'We have the most exciting views and luxurious facilities. There's a scheduled tour of the yacht, but that would be after you've settled in and other guests have arrived and properly settled in as well.' She continued.

Jersey didn't like the smile Avery was throwing at "her man", she glared at her and walked back with a frown to her duty post, keeping in mind to warn Avery off "her man".

Derrick almost chuckled as he watched Jersey walking away with that predator look in her eyes. His eyes were still focused on her ass when he remembered the lady with the most intriguing eyes standing in front of him. He turned to face her and noticed a quizzical expression on her face, he didn't know if it was because of Jersey's display or the fact that he spent more time than normal staring at Jersey's ass.

Clearing his throat, he grabbed the brochure from Avery, 'I am Derrick Peyton, nice to meet you too', he said, giving her his usual charming smile, every woman falls for it. She wasn't what you would call beautiful but she was attractive, sexy is the word, with her honey brown eyes and honey colored skin. She was 5'8 with a salivating curvy shape. He whistled lowly as he accessed her from head to toe, 'this trip was definitely going to do him some good', he thought to himself.

Still smiling, she squirmed inwardly, she bet every lady wants to get lost in those eyes and she has worked on the yacht long enough not to know people like him, spoilt, rich handsome brats, always trying to get into every girl's pant. 'Why was his name sounding familiar?' She thought and decided not to pry, if there is something she has learnt overtime, it is not to give people like this the impression that you are interested. 'Would you follow me sir, as I take you to your cabin?' She asked politely.

'Of course,' he replied, flashing a smile that showed off his white set of teeth. As she turned around and walked past him, he followed behind staring at her buttocks. He could feel his growing bulge below, damn! He wants her and he would get her. Knowing he would have a great time planning out his moves to get this sexy doll during this trip, he smiled, mischievously as he walked to his exquisite home for the next 2 months.

Philip walked out of the airport to meet a cab waiting to take him to the Atlantis yacht. The yacht was to leave in an hour, so he still had time, he thought, as he checked his wristwatch and entered the cab. He still does not feel positive about this trip, he is only doing this because Sandro kept on talking about how the trip would heal his broken heart and he wondered how that would work out though.

He has been devastated after his break up with Leticia. He used to be the best sought after photographer in Toronto and beyond not until after Leticia broke him a year ago. He has been so cold to everyone excluding Sandro who always found a way to take him out of his sorrow. His work no longer carries that extra unique touch that is peculiar to his brand. If his clients have not started complaining, they would, soon, if he does not get himself back together. Sandro has been the one keeping his head down.

What would he have done without his best friend? He sighed. Maybe he really needs this, meet new people, get new inspiration and maybe get his heart back together.

'We have gotten to your destination sir,' the cab driver

interrupted his line of thoughts.

He looked around him and saw some yachts afar, he thanked the driver, and came down from the cab, got around the car to get his luggage. He walked to the beach dragging his luggage with him, as he got to the entrance of the beach, he showed his ID to the security officer and requested for the location of the Atlantis yacht. The security officer gave him a location, Philip thanked him and walked straight to the location which he was directed to.

He walked to the yacht and entered the luxurious boat, sighting a petite blond across the counter in the room with way too much makeup on her face, flashing an irritating smile at him, He winced. Deciding to walk to her, since she seems to be the only available person in the room, he moved his legs. The moment he got to her, he saw what she was all about, 5'7 with huge breast that can jump out of their shield at any moment. She was pretty but nothing so fancy about her. Her smile was irritating him so much, he was about to talk to end his mystery before he heard her speak.

'Welcome to Atlantis, I am Jersey Jackson, you can call me J.J. Do you have a reservation here?' She asked excitedly.

So, she knew she wanted that Derrick fine man for herself, but what will it hurt to have this rugged handsome dude too? she thought as she eyed him from his silk brown hair, to his chiseled jaw line, his black shirt that was rolled up at the sleeves and denim jeans. His chest was broader than that of Derrick's and she would feel so safe and secured in his arms after a long, hard, rough sex. She thought, smiling dreamingly at him.

'Yes, I do'. He replied curtly, but cold.

'Why was he so cold?' She asked inwardly.

She knew men like this, they always played hard to get but she could deal with them perfectly, once they tasted her, they would be asking for more, she smiled knowingly to herself.

'Your reservation was made under what name sir?' She asked pushing her breast forward.

'Philip Langley', he replied impatiently, wanting to leave this scary woman already.

'Wow, Philip Langley, the biggest, finest photographer in Toronto?' She asked in a high tone, jumping up a little with her breast almost out.

He scoffed, of course he was not the biggest and finest photographer in Toronto, and he just does what he knows how to do best.

'If that's how you put. Can you please show me where I am supposed to be staying for the next 2 months as I believe this boat would be leaving the premises in what…?' he checked his wrist watch, '…20 minutes.' He said coldly with one of his fine eyebrows raised.

She was annoyed. Who does he think he is? The smile left her face replaced with a pout. She isn't leaving her duty post for this rude man.

'You can walk down the hall by your left, you will see a lady wearing the same uniform as I am, she would take you to your cabin.'

Shaking his head, he walked to the direction she pointed. He just hopes he isn't wasting his time here, the first person he met is making him harbor thoughts of turning and heading back home immediately but thinking of what Sandro would do to him if he comes back home without going through this trip, kept his feet plastered to the floor of the boat.

The moment he turned and walked to meet Avery; Jersey's eyes got glued to his perfectly shaped buttocks. The denim jeans outlined his ass and it is obvious he works out. She might keep to her initial thoughts of having this one too, even though he was annoying. She smiled mischievously.

Chapter 5- Fights and Sex

'Seriously Jeff, we haven't even started this trip and we are about to bring the boat down with our noise'. Alice lamented as she unpacked the bags in their magnificent cabin. Their room is beautiful with both a sitting room and a bedroom with just a big arch and fancy curtain dividing them and a very large beautiful bathroom. The bathroom has a shower and big bath tub, 2 radiant heat floors, heated towel rank, two-person infrared sauna and a transparent shower glass. It was the first place Alice went to check once they were left alone after that Avery stewardess showed them their place. Alice has always been a bathroom person, and the moment she saw the bathroom, her face lit up and she knew she could spend her all day in there.

The sitting room itself was another thing to talk about, starting from the big plasma TV, to the beautiful red cushions and small glass table that has underwater with small yellow fishes inside, sitting at the center of the sitting room. Everything was mesmerizing, including the king-sized bed and big wardrobe in the bedroom. The moment they arrived, Jeffery went to put on the TV and switched to the sport channel, they've always had an argument on TV channels and Alice has always disliked anything sport and currently this was the cause of the argument.

'Thank God, you said it yourself', Jeffrey interjected with his hands raised in air and a sigh leaving his mouth.

'I am not saying you shouldn't watch whatever, but don't just think when my favorite shows are on, I will sit with you and watch that rubbish' Alice retorted.

'Don't call what I am watching rubbish!' He shouted getting frustrated already.

'I would call it rubbish because it is rubbish!' She shouted back.

He stood up swiftly, and walked towards her in angry strides to the bedroom where she was unpacking, the look in his eyes were scary at the same time stimulating.

'Al', he said dangerously while looking down at her, she was supposed to feel scared or something but hell, she was so horny just staring at the fire in his eyes.

'Okay, fine!' She huffed, looking down at their clothes and wondering what was wrong with her, 'It is still rubbish', she mumbled lowly with her head faced down not because she wanted to continue the argument but because she wanted to hear his voice again and feel the squeeze of her kitten. Okay, she needs to be fucked!

'What did you say?' he asked in a very low dangerous tone, he knew what she was doing because he felt it too. It has been so long since they've been together physically, sleeping in the same bed and not touching, how did he survive? Maybe sexual tension is one of the reasons for all these little arguments. Since they decided to totally avoid each other a year ago, when things got really bad between them, they've not had sex not to talk about love making.

This is not the place or time to do whatever was running through their heads, so she decided to push it away, 'Jeff, let's just stop arguing, we have just an hour 30 minutes, to settle in and freshen up for group tour' she said with her eyes boring into his. 'And dear husband, there are some famous guests in this yacht with us, so let's put on our best behavior once we are outside', she said smiling sweetly at him, knowing he might try to bring out an argument from her last statement.

Jeffery sighed, he was about to object to her last statement until he saw the smile on her face, he was a sucker for her smiles, he doesn't even know why she doesn't use it against him during their arguments. 'Yeah, fine', he said grudgingly and headed to the bathroom to take a long shower, he really hopes this trip is worth it because a day had not passed and he was already tired.

The yacht left the shore at exactly 14:00hours America time. The guests have settled in their various cabins and would be out for their group tour in an hour time. Jersey decided she had nothing to do at the welcome room, she needed to take care of her needs. She called Emily, the Russian stewardess and pleaded with her to stay at her post so she can help answer the intercom when any of the guests needs something.

Emily is a sweet lady in her mid-thirties, she knew what Jersey had up her sleeves but she would let have her way this time, after all she currently has nothing to do. She was in charge of making sure every cabin was neatly cleaned and arranged before the arrival of the guests and during their stay in the yacht. Currently everyone is in their room, so she is free and that is the only reason she would stand in for her. Jersey thanked her and hurried down to the yacht's lounge.

Garret was in charge of the lounge; he and Jersey has been hitting off since they started working at Atlantis yacht. It was just sex, rough, hard sex. That was it, no love-like-feeling of any sort between them. They were just physically attracted to each other and found a way to release sexual tension off each other when they are not screwing any guests on the yacht. Garret was 6'1 with a slender figure, he has blue eyes that shimmer when he gets to his cloud 9 during sex, figured out by Jersey.

He isn't exactly what you would call handsome, but Jersey could use him to get her release instead of touching herself at night and his crooked smile turns her on every damn time. She walked straight to him, smiling sweetly.

'Hey baby', she purred.

He raised his heads from the book he was scribbling on and gave her his crooked smile. She was so wet, after her encounter with Derrick Peyton and that cold photographer, she couldn't sit well without squirming on her chair or squeezing her legs together. She walked across the counter and pulled him with his shirt, she had no time for foreplay, she wanted to get this damn tension from her body.

He laughed, 'Are you that hungry?' He asked in a low sexy voice, which made her shiver a little, she needs to be fucked hard badly!

'Garret, I have no time for this and besides the guest would soon be out in less than an hour, can you take care of this little kitten in that short time?' She whined seductively. Garret needed no more persuasion; he was hot for her already. He pulled her roughly to the store room behind the lounge.

The moment they got to the store room, he yanked the front of her shirt down, revealing two very large sumptuous nipples he likes to feed on, he wasted no time in plunging them into his ready mouths at the same time searching for her wet kitten with his fingers, he found it and inserted two of his fingers, causing her to moan out loudly.

Jersey didn't care if anyone was passing by, she just wanted her needs taken care of. 'Baby I need to feel you inside of me', she cried. His cock was struggling to jump out of his pants, so he released her breast from his mouth and began fondling them with his hand, turning her around against wall, while using his free hand to release his cock, preparing it to enter her.

He lifted her skirts, 'Do you want daddy to fuck you hard? Do you want him to make you squirt so hard you can't walk? Do you want all of daddy?!' He growled. She nodded eagerly, struggling to talk, it was like she would combust if he doesn't enter her at that moment.

'Daddy wants to hear you'. He said with a strained voice, positioning himself at the entrance of her kitten. She couldn't take it anymore, she almost screamed, 'Yes daddy! I want you to fuck me so hard I can't walk'. She cringed inwardly, if she can't walk well after this episode, that manager would have her head for dinner, before she lost herself in this immense pleasure, she said, 'Daddy, just remember we both have work to do after this'.

He laughed as he entered her with one powerful trust, whatever she wanted to say got stocked up in her throat. She would enjoy this moment and think later. They both rode each other till they could no longer pronounce any sensible English word.

Chapter 6 – Coy Leonard

Clara was excited to be on this trip, she just walked out of her cabin to join the others for a group tour. The tour wasn't compulsory, but it was necessary, if not 'why are you here?' She thought to herself. When she was given the brochure, she waited till she got to her room before she went through it, the pictures of the lounge, spa, gym and so many more excited her beyond words, not to talk about the services they render.

It's not like she doesn't have her time in expensive lounges or spa back home, but engaging in those same activities in Atlantis yacht with so much freedom of not being perfect, especially in the eyes of her mother, made her feel lighter than she had in years, after all, most persons here are famous people like her that came to enjoy themselves, so there would be no need to act all perfect, she smiled to herself as she walked down to meet the tour guide and the rest of the guest.

'Welcome ladies and gents, I am Stefano Williams, I would be your tour guide for this evening. I want you to feel free to ask me any question whatsoever and please enjoy the view'. He said with a boyish grin. Stefano is a crew member on the yacht and was always enthusiastic to do this particular job. They were all on the lower deck of yacht and he would start his tour from their current location.

Clara looked around and she could see there was a couple amongst them, a southern middle-aged man, wait, is that Toronto's finest photographer?! Philip Langley? Wow, she couldn't believe he was here. He is a very famous photographer; in fact, he is one of the best she has worked with. She kept on assessing the other guests as the tour guard walked them around the deck. She noticed a very striking handsome man, walking with a string of arrogance, his face looks so familiar but she couldn't place a name to him at that moment, she would probably find out more about him before she leaves here, she thought.

'...this is the lower deck and all guest cabins are located here, there is an exterior swimming pool at the stern, an engine room amidships and the crew quarters. No guest is allowed in the engine room or in the crew quarters. There is an intercom in every room, so when you need the attention of any of the crew, you advised to…' the tour guide continued.

Clara wondered if the room intercoms were in perfect working condition, alongside all amenities in her room, so she would not have any need to come out looking for any crew member. She was about to ask this question when they were moved from the quarters to the exterior swimming pool and the thing she was about to say got trapped in her throat,

'Gosh, this pool is breathtaking'. She softly said as she gave a little gasp.

'Isn't it?' she heard a rough voice say beside her, she turned to sight the warmest dark brown eyes she has ever seen.' I am Coy Leonard, and it is refreshing to see someone appreciates the pool as much as much as I do' he drawled with an Italian accent and gave her a warm smile, she almost turned and hugged him.

She gave him a small smile, 'I am Clara Davis, nice to meet you too.'

There was something about him, she didn't meet her father before he died, so she had always missed a father figure in her life, apart from her uncle that takes that space in her life, even though he is not always available, Clara doesn't know what it means to have a father. But looking at this man, she feels like a daughter, she shook those thoughts off her head, what was she thinking? Few hours on the boat and her emotions are already on high alert, she sighed as she walked with the others to the main deck of the yacht.

Coy is an experienced traveler, he has travelled almost everywhere in the world. He is a 57-year-old man of 5'9 and has had two divorces in the space of 12 years with no children. His last marriage ended when he was 37, he was young and inexperienced when he married his first wife, Mel. They had so many issues, they decided to go their separate ways, until he met his second wife, Tricia, still young and naive, he ventured into another marriage and after 4 years, it ended.

He was so distraught and decided to travel round the world to meet new people and study the lives of people especially couples, he picked up a lot of knowledge moving around and was able to figure the mistakes he made during his marriage. He pushed out the thoughts of marriage and enjoyed seeing new places and meeting new people.

Now he was on this yacht because he heard it was heading to Palawan Islands and he wanted to visit that Island for a long time now, not because he couldn't fly down there all alone but the thought of using a super yacht as luxurious as Atlantis yacht and meeting new people intrigued him beyond words and he decided to try it, after all he has all the money he could spend.

Smiling down up at Clara, he was glad he came.

They were on the main deck and Coy was awed by the structure of the deck. He listened to the guide as he has been speaking since they got there, '...dining room, spa, beauty salon, lounge and a glass-enclosed gym are right here on the main deck, we have an outdoor dining at the deck, that's if you don't want to use the one here. Our gallery is filled with art crafts and paintings from different parts of the world, most especially from Africa'. The guide explained with his eyes lit up.

He took them to each of the spots mentioned and they were all in awe of the views they were been exposed to. Next, they moved to the upper deck where they were showed the outdoor dining, movie theater, the captain's cabin and that of the yacht's manager and a medical room. They got to know that the yacht had some amenities stored for pleasure and movement to use ashore, two motor scooters, two-seater automobile, jet skis, kayaks, sailboats, diving and fishing gear, and water skis were among the things the tour guide showed to them.

Moving to the Sun deck, which is the uppermost deck on yacht, they were shown a hot tub and a sky lounge. Coy thought about how much time he would spend here, as this seems to be his favorite view, it was like standing on the boat and viewing the world from there, with a sense of serenity. Oh yes, this was definitely a good idea, he thought.

Philip moved around with the tour guide and other guests, he felt his excitement building up, it wasn't what he was expecting even though he had heard about the Atlantis yacht, he didn't know it was this grand. It was a sight to behold and at that moment, he began to eliminate the thought of the trip not been worthwhile.

The most intriguing place to him was the uppermost deck, where there was a sky lounge, in fact the thought of sitting at the lounge there, having an unrestricted view of the sky and big sea while he thinks away his sorrow was like solace to him, he thought as he looked around with a smile at the corner of his mouth.

Ha hasn't taken out time to look at the other guests since the tour begun, so he used this opportunity to scan them with his gray eyes, his eyes widened as they fell on Clara Davis. How come he didn't see her till now, with her eyes as blue and clearer as the sky and her hair that wasn't hard to miss? Simple, his mind wasn't really there, he sighed as he walked up to her.

'Clara?' He asked with a smile on his face and his eyes boring into hers, he has always loved her eyes, they carried a lot of mystery, yet they were kind. Clara was a cold person and hardly says more than few words in hours, but working with her over the years has equipped him with the ability to make her talk and bring out that lovely part of her he knew she was hiding.

The moment Clara heard her name, she turned and found herself staring at Philip, she felt like someone who was caught with her hand in the cookie jar, seeing him earlier, she knew she was at least supposed to greet him or something, but she ignored it, waving the greeting till after the tour. Truth be told, Philip has a way of seeing way too much than she wants, she talks more than she should when she was with him during shoots and she didn't like it one bit. She didn't have friends and she would like keep it that way, that was why she was reluctant to let him know she was there.

'Hi Philip', She said politely without even the tiniest smile, Philip knew her and his smile just widened, she hasn't changed one bit.

'Why do I have a feeling you saw me earlier before I saw you now?' He asked with a smirk.

'Maybe if you didn't wander into your wonderland as usual, you would have seen me earlier', she retorted. Philip used to be a very jovial person when she started working with him on a contract deal, she signed with Pearl Naturelle skin care brand in Toronto, that was 2 years ago before he started acting so dull and get lost in his thoughts until someone pulls him out. She knew it wasn't her business, but was curious as to what happened to change his demeanor that way, but knowing the way she operated, she minded her business.

He knew what she was talking about, obviously his best friend wasn't the only one that knew about his depressing attitude of spacing out even when he was in the midst of people.

'Well, that doesn't answer my question', he said with one of his eyebrows raised up.

Feigning a gasp, 'Sorry, did you ask me a question?' She asked while struggling not to smile.

Philip chuckled, keeping one hand in his pocket and stretching out the other one to her, 'Nice to meet you here beautiful Clara Davis, and I hope you didn't come here with your "Ice Queen" coat,', he said with a grin while stressing on "Ice Queen".

She took his hand and smiled this time around, he always insisted no matter how she much denied that she had an invincible "Ice Queen" coat she carries around with her, that's why her face never breaks into a smile. So she always smiles when he says that to prove him wrong.

'For the thousandth time Philip, I don't have any coat like that in my closet, hope you have a nice stay here too', she said with a smile and ended the handshake.

He nodded and flashed his perfect set of teeth, 'See more of you Clara'.

Staring at him, she saw it has been so long she saw his smile reach his eyes the way it was now, she wonders how he can have any problem big enough to wipe the contagious light in his eyes. He was very successful and amazingly handsome, she bet he has a lot of girls fighting to get in bed with him, she might even be among those girls, if her life was anything close to normal.

'Uh, sorry but I am going to be too busy blinding you with my smiles, you might not be able to see me', she smirked, as she turned to the guide who announced to them that it was time to go back to their cabins as dinner would be served in an hour and they would have a little party to welcome them, while hiding a smile from Philip.

He laughed, quietly enough not to draw the attention of the other guest and shook his head. He didn't even say much and she was already coming back at him with witty remarks. He would certainly see more of her, maybe he could do with a friend while he spends his next 3 months on the beautiful yacht.

Avery was running around helping the chef to set dining room before the guests arrive for dinner. Since they were having an extraordinaire dinner cum party, they would be using the external dining room at the upper deck. The crew had taken their time to make sure everything was in place, it wasn't an elaborate party, but it was just created for the guests to familiarize with each other and have little fun before they retired to bed.

Everything I wanted by Billie Elish, was playing softly through the speakers in the room. While nodding her head to the music, she walked to the table with the menu in her hands and placed each one in a way every person that would sit on the table would have a copy to themselves.

After that little task, she moved back and stared around, everything was in order, the small bell at the table to draw the attention of any of the stewardess, the white table wears, the dishes, glass and cutleries, the candle lights that haven't been switched on yet, the bottles of champagne, the bucket of ice, and the beautiful flower on the middle of the table. All was set according to exquisite taste and class.

She was serving alongside Emily tonight and she was eager, she loved her job, it pays her well and gave her the opportunity to see new places, meet new people and learn new things. She stood at the staircase that connected the decks together to welcome any guest that walks in, while Emily was at the table to serve their drinks and get them settled before dinner starts.

It wasn't long before she sensed a presence at the stairs and as she raised her head to welcome the person, her eyes connected with the handsome photographer she encountered hours ago. She felt lost again, earlier when he walked up to her to get the direction of his cabin, he wasn't even smiling like the first guest that approached her. He was cold, he didn't look even look at her, just mumbled out his name and received the brochure, she could see he was handsome but she didn't get to see his face not until they stopped at his cabin and he looked up at her to say thank you. That was all it took, she got lost.

Her breath hitched in her throat, her feet were plastered to the ground and her mouth was slightly opened, at that moment it felt like she was breathing through her mouth. She couldn't even tell what was going on with her, but staring at him, she felt something stirred deep inside of her. It when she saw his left eye twitch, or maybe she imagined it that was when she realized where she was and what she was doing, she scurried away and promised herself that wouldn't happen again.

Now she was here, staring at this man, lost again. His hazel eyes were captivating, they held so much, yet they looked empty, he was wearing a perfectly ironed white shirt, with the sleeves cuffed securely at his wrists, she could see his broad chest and huge muscles threatening to jump out, making her mouth dry, his dark blue pants smugly resting across his long legs, his brown silk hair stopping at the nape of his neck, his full brown eyebrows, pointy nose, full mouth and the silver earring on his left ear winking at her. She felt hot just staring at him, damn she has not seen a better ruggedly handsome man than the one in front of her, she felt the stirring in her stomach again, and there she knew she was going to have a problem having this man around.

She stood there for what felt like hours, even though it was just seconds, until she heard him cleared his throat and returned back to earth, she didn't know if she could utter a word without stuttering, but she had to say something.

'Welcome sir, please move to the table over there, you would be attended to by a stewardess. Hope you have a lovely dinner', she said with a surprisingly strong voice, she was proud of herself. He walked past her with a nod and she turned and looked at him, she shook her head and whispered to herself, 'Keep it together girl'.

How is going? I hope that you are enjoying. It took me a while to imagine and create this story.

Leave a short review on Amazon if you enjoy it.

https://www.amazon.com/review/create-review

Chapter 7 - Feelings

Philip walked to the dining table and sat down with a frown on his face, deep in thoughts, he didn't even hear a thing the stewardess said, until he heard, '...can you hear me? Excuse me sir?' in a thick Russian accent pulling him away from his thoughts, causing him to raise his heads to the direction from where the sound came.

'Can you please go through the menu and let me know what you'd be having, sir?' She said, gesturing to the menu in front of him.

He nodded and picked up the menu, letting his eyes scan through it while silently scolding himself from being so absent minded, but he couldn't really concentrate. This was the second time that girl was staring at him like that, but what got him bothered wasn't her stares but what he felt looking back at her. She was very attractive, no doubt, and has a warm voice but there is just something he couldn't quite place his hands on, looking at her back there, he had this strange feeling that he could share his pains and problems with her and she would give him comfort, he felt like he has known he for so long, it felt nostalgic.

But how can he feel that way about somebody he just met? Someone he hasn't even uttered more than 5 words to?, he can remember when he met her to give him the direction to his cabin, he didn't want any conversation just like he had with that Jersey girl, he just wanted to get to his room and have his personal space for a moment, she had spoken so cheerful and polite, yet he didn't bother looking at her until his good manners kicked in when they got to the door of his cabin and he decided to look at her and say thank you and that was when he felt that flutter in his heart and the reaction he gave out was the twitching of his left eyes, which happens often when he felt nervous. It wasn't the attraction that disturb him, it was the nostalgic feeling he felt, but he waved it off there and then.

Now this night, he took his time to access her and realized how sexy she looked even on her uniform, he is a photographer and he has seen a lot of sexy and more beautiful ladies, but there was still this thing that was pulling him to her and making his heart soften, so he didn't trust his voice enough not reveal anything, that was why when she spoke to him, he didn't say anything and just walked away with a nod.

'Sir, have you picked anything yet?' the stewardess said interrupting his thoughts again.

Realizing he had spaced out again, he looked at her with pleading eyes, 'just a minute ma'am', he said as he looked back at the menu. Scanning through the menu, he saw a lot of dishes on display and his eyes found what he wanted.

'I would have the chicken with feta cheese, dill, lemon and Harissa yogurt', he said as he handed the menu to her and gave her a smile.

'Alright, that would be ready in a couple of minutes. Would you like me to pour you a glass of champagne while you wait for your meal?' She inquired.

'Yes, please', he said. She raised the glass from the table, popped up the champagne and poured a reasonable amount of wine for him.

'Thank you …?' he asked, trying to get her name.

She looked at him and smiled, of course she knew he hasn't been listening to half of the things she has been saying, whatever was making him space out like that wasn't a small issue, 'Emily Fedya', she said, as those thoughts ran through her mind.

'Emily Fedya', he repeated realizing she was Russian. She walked away and he looked up at the table, that was when he realized he wasn't alone, there was a couple speaking in low raspy voice across him, he wondered what they were whispering about, deciding to keep to himself, he wandered into his thoughts.

One of his favorite songs, *your love keeps lifting me* by Jackie Wilson, was playing softly from the speakers in the dining room and Alice won't allow him to enjoy the song. He just walked from their cabin with Alice and she was currently rattling in his ears of how he has lost his gentleman manners.

Their heads slightly bowed to each other, 'You see where most of our problems are coming from?' Alice quietly asked with a stern voice.

'Where?' Jeffery asked in a low voice too.

'You didn't pull the chair out for me to sit, you just sat down, ignoring me. You are supposed to be a gentleman but you aren't any longer, this is the reason we have so many fights', she hissed out.

'I didn't ignore you Al, hell, you even sat down before I did. Why are you even making this an argument?' He questioned, getting agitated as they weren't the only ones at the table and they were beginning to draw attention to themselves.

'It wouldn't have been an argument, if you had done what you were supposed to do or at least apologized for your behavior', she fired, all the while speaking in low tones.

He looked at her and wondered why she was like this, he knew it wasn't the fact that he didn't pull out the chair that was working her up, he would try to keep them together, till they were alone in their rooms.

'I am sorry', he said softly while looking into her eyes, 'we have an audience already, let's not create a scene' he said pleading with his eyes.

She looked up and noticed the dinning was almost filled up, she nodded and straightened her back against the chair. Something was eating at her, she was hurt, it wasn't because Jeffery did not pull out the chair, it was something else. Earlier on, she walked out of the bedroom nervously, looking up at Jeffery for a compliment to ease her nerves, he just looked up and said 'let's go'.

She was putting on a knee length black dress with no straps and a silver 5 inches heels with matching dangling earrings, her makeup was very light but flawless, it has been a while she dressed up that way but she felt beautiful, eager for Jeff to at least make a compliment, all he said was 'let's go'.

Her thoughts were disturbed by one the stewardess, 'What would you like to take ma'am?' She said with a warm voice.

Alice looked up at the menu, her appetite was lost already so she looked at her husband and saw he was waiting for her to decide. 'Anything he picks', she shrugged as she gestured to her husband.

The Russian stewardess smiled with a nod and diverted her attention to Jeffery, leaving her to wallow in her thoughts.

Doesn't he find me attractive anymore? Do I irritate him? Do I look fat? Why didn't he say something about my look tonight? Come to think of it when last did he compliment me? He hasn't even touched me in a long while now, all these questions where dancing through her head, she didn't even know if she could go through with this dinner.

Jeffery looked at Alice, the frown was evident on her face, and something else he couldn't put a name to was definitely wrong with her, he was worried and didn't know how to comfort her, he did the only thing he could think of at that moment, he found one of her hands and gave it a squeeze, the squeeze communicating what his words couldn't at that moment.

She felt him squeeze her hand and she felt a little better, she promised herself there and then that she won't worry about a thing, she would enjoy this evening with this wonderful people and think about her problems later. Once she came to that conclusion, she did what she knew how to do best, she has always been a social person , she would be herself on this table, she decided as picked up a glass and clanked it gently with a fork, drawing the attention of everyone to herself.

'Can I have your attention please?' she said with a smile, 'Thank you' she continued, when she saw everyone shifting their gaze to her. 'I believe this is like a meet and greet dinner party, can we at least get to know each other before our dinner arrives', she announced cheerfully, hearing a murmur of agreement across the room, she continued.

'You can start with your names, what you do and what city you came from…,' without taking a pause she said with a bright smile, 'I am Alice Myron and this is my husband Jeffery Myron..', she said pointing to her husband sitting beside her, who in turn nodded with a smile, '… My husband is one of the best defense attorneys in the city and I own the popular Looks by Al makeup studio in New York City'. She proudly said.

She noticed how the southern middle aged man sitting across her, began clapping before others joined him. She grinned and winked at him.

She got to know his name was Coy Leonard and he was a traveler that explained the switch in accents as he talked to everyone. He was wise and had a lot of things to say, even made everyone laughed in just a short time, Alice observed.

The introduction continued until, Clara introduced herself as a model and mentioned the fact that she was from Moscow.

'Do you speak any Russian?' Coy asked Clara with a smile.

'Yes, I do but I haven't in a long while so my Russian is a bit rusty', she replied.

He nodded, before he could say any other thing, Derrick, the son of the automobile distributor blurted out, 'I speak Russian',

'Really?' Coy questioned with his brows raised up and a grin on his face.

'Yeah, I grew up in St. Petersburg, but schooled in one of the best colleges in London', he answered with a cocky grin making Clara roll her eyes.

Before the conversation could get heightened, one of the stewardess announced to them that dinner was about to be served, she dim the light in the room, lighted the candles and changed the song on the music player to Eric Clapton's *wonderful tonight.*

The stewards and stewardess matched into the room with different dishes ordered by the guests. They placed each of the dishes requested by the guests including desserts on the table. Avery announced to them that they would be having, chocolate cookie skillet, caramel apple tart and lemon pound cake for dessert.

Alice squealed on hearing the lemon pound cake for dessert, she loves cakes, any kind of cake. She looked down to see what her husband ordered for dinner and she wasn't disappointed as she saw, sweet potato noodles with chorizo, roasted red pepper and spinach on her plate.

She took a sip of her wine and went ahead to devour the sumptuous sight that was before her. She was going to enjoy her night she thought as the conversations bubbled over the table.

Avery excused herself from the rest to the quarters, she shares it with Emily, Jersey and Matilda the shy new girl. She was exhausted, she knew the first dinner parties are usually one of the most stressful as everyone switches duty to give the guest a classy and exquisite dinner, except the chef who concentrates on cooking and the captain who sails the boat, the manager too is always available for occasions like this to supervise and make sure everywhere is in order. Camila, the manager was always of the option that 'First impression matters a lot', so most times, they always out-do themselves and come out with tremendous results at the end.

She yawns while stretching her body, she left the girls gossiping in the kitchen, talking about how handsome Derrick and the photographer was, she moved to them to join in the conversation, but the moment she heard them talking about the photographer, she excused herself and scurried hurriedly to bed not trusting herself to close her mouth during the discussion.

Now in the room, she peeled off her clothes, piece by piece until she was butt naked, she walked into the bathroom, put on the shower, and the moment the water hit her, a sigh left her lips, she was so grateful for the inventor of this particular shower.

Spending less than 20 minutes in shower, Avery came out with a towel around her hair and another around her body, scanning the room, she noticed the girls weren't back yet. She peeled the towel from her body, walked to the mirror admiring her curves, went through with usual night routine, putting on a tank top and pajamas short, Avery descended on her bunk bed with a slump.

It wasn't until she shut her eyes, did she hear the giggles of the girls as they nosily walked into the room causing her to squirm deeper under her blankets. Soon, Avery was drifting into sleep with the face of one person in her mind.

Chapter 8 - Impressions and Expressions

They have been on the sea for two weeks now and Philip didn't think he was getting better, in fact, he noticed he spaced out more often than before, but this time around it wasn't Leticia that occupied his thoughts, it was this Avery girl. He found himself rolling over the bed thinking about her every night.

Every time he sees her, something happens to him, he just wants to walk up to her, stare into her eyes and let out his problems to her. He needs to get a grip on himself, he can't let another girl into his heart, never. Leticia thought him a lesson and he would learn from it, he decided as he consciously tried to erase Avery's face from his head, which was almost impossible.

He was in the sky lounge having whiskey. He had decided to wander off to the lounge after dinner to clear his head. He was the only one there when he heard some shuffling from the entrance, looking up, he couldn't put a face to the figure walking to him, that was when he realized he was a little bit tipsy, he never takes more than two shots, but he has taken three already and he's not sure he would be able to stop at three, he needed to kill the pain in his heart and clear his head.

'Do you need anything sir?' he heard the figure say as it drew closer. It became clearer and he realized who she was, he didn't need this now, he groaned inwardly.

'No, I am fine', he replied coldly.

She took a step closer towards him, 'I can see you are here alone; can I at least join you?' She asked in a low seductive tone.

'Thank you for your offer Jersey, but no!' He said.

She sat down across him regardless of his reply, he saw how short her skirts were and the three buttons of her shirt were open, revealing her cleavages to anyone who cared to see.

'You know, sometimes you might not really know what you want until you've had it', she purred.

He looked at her as he felt his head sway, what the hell was wrong with this girl? Can't she see he wasn't interested? He knew what she wanted and ever since Leticia, he hasn't had sex with any other person, no matter how much Sandro pressured him, the thought of sleeping with someone else irritated him.

'What do you want?' he coldly asked.

She smiled sweetly, 'I want you to see me', she said while releasing more buttons on her shirt.

He looked at what she displayed to him, he slightly shook his head, the alcohol was already working its magic.

'Don't you have work to do?' he asked with a frown on his face.

'I am all yours baby', she whispered, thinking she has finally gotten his attention.

Philip knew he wasn't the least interested, but maybe if he slept with her he could take Leticia off his system, he thought. She was batting her lashes at him, while pushing the hem of her skirt higher.

Jersey thought she was getting to him, as she sat across him and watched the numerous expressions play out on his fine face. Maybe she wouldn't spend tonight with the girls but with this man, in those strong arms, she thought, as she stood up from where she sat and walked up to him seductively, placing her fingers on his arms.

The moment he felt her hand on his bare skin, he jerked away, causing her to pull away, he was putting on a short sleeved black t-shirt and when she placed her fingers on the exposed skin of his arms, he felt like she stung him. He needs her to leave now. He picked up his glass, and gulped down the remaining content.

His head was pounding and this girl was making it worst, 'Leave', he said in a low but strong voice.

When he jerked away, she thought she was breaking down his defense, so she smiled to herself and as she was about to touch him again, she heard him say 'Leave', maybe she didn't hear him right, she decided to try again, this time around she would extend her fingers to his strong chest, she thought.

'Leave!' he said again, this time around it was loud and harsh.

She was startled, what was wrong with this man?

'Do you want me to leave?' She asked with a pout

'Yes! Please leave!' he almost barked, he was losing his patience, he knew all she wanted was just to sleep with him and get his money. He was tired of women always trying to use him. He was suffocating, he needed to breath, everything was coming at him all at once, the alcohol was making things worst and he needed this girl out of here.

Jersey looked at him confused, wasn't he acting interested some minutes ago? What did she do wrong? She knew she was good when it comes to making men fall for her, but this man was playing stubborn. Deciding to try again, she bent down, pushing her breast into his face, she raised her knee and was about to place her hands on his crotch.

'Get out!' he shouted with so much force causing her to hurriedly walk away with her eyes as wide as a scared cat, he scared her so much, she ran straight to the quarters without bothering to button up her shirts.

The moment she was out of sight, he slumped back into the chair, he was devastated, everything kept rushing back at him, how much he loved Leticia, how much he could do anything for her but she decided to pay him back the way she did. How every woman he met just wanted to use him for their benefit, how hurt he was, he couldn't even heal after one year, how this Avery girl wont just leave his mind. His head was spinning, he couldn't get a hold of himself, he picked up the glass on the table and threw it across the room with a stifled cry. All he could see was blood as he slumped back to the chair with his head in his palms.

Avery was on the upper deck, she just finished with laundry and was about to go to the quarters when she saw Jersey climbing down and running pass her with her buttons open and her hair flying around her like her pants caught fire. She was amused and curious at the same time and decided to walk to the direction Jersey came from, to see what made her the way she was.

She got to the upper most deck, seeing nobody, she moved to the lounge, knowing she would find the young steward at the bar, maybe something happened between him and Jersey, she thought. As she got to the lounge, she heard a muffled cry and glass went flying everywhere.

She quickly got cover to prevent the glass from touching her, after some seconds, she looked up at the direction from which the glass flew from and noticed the silhouette of a man sitting on one of the sofas with his head in his palms. His body was shaking and it was like he was crying or trying not to cry.

She couldn't make sense of what was happening, so she looked at the bar counter to get answers from the young steward there only to see him wide eye opened with a terrified expression on his face. Seeing him like that, she pitied him, knowing he would have to clean up the place before morning. She walked up to him.

'What happened here?' She asked.

He looked up from the scene before him and looked at her, noticing he wasn't alone, he hurriedly picked up the magazine from the counter and threw it under. Avery had a glimpse of the magazine before he picked it, there was a display of a naked woman on it, shaking her head, she knew he doesn't know what happened and was probably jerking off at the back of the counter before the incident.

'I …uh...um……the', he stammered.

'Just leave, I would take it from here', she interrupted him.

He was about to say something again, when she raised one of hands, 'Goodnight Leo, I can handle it,' she said.

He nodded and bent down to adjust himself before he scurried out of the lounge. Once he left, Avery looked at the pieces of the shattered glass, then at the man and sighed. 'Let's do this', she whispered to nobody in particular as she picked up the brooms from the back of the bar counter and began to work.

Philip sat down there for so long he couldn't remember. He was breathing so hard trying not to cry. He was drunk and hurt. It was like no matter how much he drank; the pains won't go away. He decided to steady himself before he went back to his cabin. He didn't want anyone to see him in his current state, so he decided to stay long into the night till he was sure everyone was in bed before he left.

He was bleeding, but he didn't care, he was so numb he couldn't feel the pains from the cut on his hands, cuts from the glass he broke. He heard some shuffling, like someone was sweeping and cleaning, cleaning up his mess, he felt really guilty and decided to apologize to the person for his actions.

He lifted his head, and his eyes connected to Avery's eyes, was he seeing things now? Were his imaginations coming to reality? He questioned himself with his brows furrowed looking up at Avery. He saw the look of surprise on her face, it changed to longing, and then she quickly looked away and continued with what she was doing.

He felt hurt, guilty and ashamed. Why did she look away? Why was she here? Why is she the one cleaning up his mess? Why did she have to be the one to see him in this state? All these questions ran through his mind as he sat back and watched her work.

She has been avoiding him for the past two weeks, since that first dinner party. Even when she needed to clean his cabin and change his bedspread, she found a way to bribe Emily to do the job. Whenever his thoughts came up in her head, she would try to push it away until she was left alone in her bed at night, when it was difficult not to think about those eyes that held so much but still looked empty.

Now here she was, staring down at the face of the man that has refused to leave her mind since this trip started. She was surprised to find out he was the one sitting there, but then when he looked at her, she knew something was wrong, all she wanted to do at that moment was to soothe him, make his pains go away, but she couldn't, so she looked away.

Avery quickly and nervously cleaned up the mess knowing he was watching her all through. Packing up to leave and struggling not to look at him, she noticed the dripping of blood at his feet from the corner of her left eye, she turned to him and traced the blood stain with her eyes to his hands.

Why isn't he making an attempt to clean his cut? She asked herself as she realized he probably got the cuts from the broken glass. She dropped what she was holding and quickly ran to the medical room to get a first aid box. She was back in less than 5 minutes, walked up straight to him, knelt down in front of him while she opened the box pulling out a disinfectant, cotton wool and a small bandage, knowing he silently watched what she was doing.

'Give me your hand', she said in a soft voice.

Still staring at her without moving, her voice was so warm, he didn't know how to react.

'You are bleeding and I would have to clean the floor, but I can't do it with the blood still dripping out', She spoke again causing him to look at the floor and see the mess he had created again.

'Thank you, I will take it up from here', he said.

'I insist', she quietly said looking up at him, the look in his eyes pulling at her heart.

He sighed, and then stretched out his hand to her, when she took it in those small hands of her, he felt a jolt inside of him, it was so strong he almost pulled back his hand and he knew she felt it too, because she paused for a second before she continued to take care of his cut.

Avery cleaned and placed a small bandage across the cut on his left palm while she packed back the tools, she just used into the first aid box, conscious of the fact that he has been accessing her all this while.

'Why are you doing this?' he asked suddenly breaking the silence in the room.

'Because I want to help', She replied.

'Why do you want to help?' he asked.

She stood up from her position and looked into his blood-shot red eyes, looking at the table, she saw the empty bottle of whiskey. He might be drunk, so she might as well say what was on her mind, maybe he won't remember after tonight, she thought.

Shrugging, she said, 'I really don't know, you look sad and something about you keeps pulling at me, I see you and I just want to do anything to take that sadness away'. She hopes she has not revealed too much.

He didn't know if he heard her well, he knew he was tipsy but he was still aware of what was happening around him. She wants to take his sadness away? He scoffed, he has had enough, and who does she think she is? He needs to get to bed now, he concluded as he tried to get up, but the minute he did, his head began spinning and he was about to fall back into the chair when he felt a warm hand but strong hand wiggle around his waist to steady his balance.

The instant he realized whose hand it belonged to, he jerked away, making his head hurt the more.

'I can take care of myself', he said harshly pulling away from her.

'I know you can take care of yourself, but let me help, it's obvious the alcohol is slowing you down', she retorted.

'I don't need you to help me, just go, I can walk myself', he said in a more harsh tone.

She doesn't know what she said wrong but she won't back down, she thought as she pulled one of his hands and snaked it around her neck. 'I am going to help you to your door, you can take it from there', she said with determination.

Seeing she wasn't backing down, he heaved a sigh and let her have her way, besides he really couldn't walk to his cabin without tripping off or causing harm to himself. She walked him to the door of his cabin and was about to step away from him when he pulled her close to his body causing air to wheeze out of her body.

She looked up to see why he did what he did only for her to get lost in his eyes. They lost track of time, they just stood there staring at each other afraid to breathe. Philip began moving his head closer to hers, his gaze directed on her full lips, she could feel his hot breathe on her face, she forgot how to breathe, her eyes were on his lips too and all it took was for him to move his head another 2 inches and she would be in wonderland.

Then she remembered he was tipsy, and would probably regret it the next day, she had to do the right thing, she cleared her throat and slightly pushed him away, he released her still staring.

'Goodnight sir', she whispered and hurried to her room, leaving him there, staring at her, was like the hardest thing she had to do in a longest time now.

Chapter 9 – Clara and Derrick

Derrick smiled as he saw Jersey walked pass him with a slight limp that might not be noticeable if you don't look well. He remembered how she moaned out his name repeatedly last night. He was walking into his cabin when he saw her running with her breasts almost flying out of her shirt, as almost all the buttons were off, the sight aroused him and he took what he wanted at that moment, she was about running past him when he stretched out his arm and paused her run.

Before she could release the scream in her throat, he quickly pulled her to him, and took her into his cabin. When she realized who it was, she melted into his arms. He kissed her, yanked off her bra, took hold of her breasts and stuffed one of them into his mouth, turning her screams into moans. He yanked off every piece of clothing from her and fucked her senseless. He banged into her so hard and rough, he was scared the other guests would hear her screams and moans. He was frustrated and it took it all out on her, he had just ended a call with his father telling him to return as fast as possible to resume his position as the CEO in the company when he saw Jersey and decided to release the tension he felt.

He gave her some money after the fuck, hell he gave her $300, why is she avoiding his eyes and acting like he didn't just fuck her last night? He wondered as he relaxed deeper into the water. She can do whatever she wants, he has gotten what he wanted, he thought with a smirk on his face.

He came to the swimming pool this hot afternoon to relax and clear his head, he was lying in the water with just his upper body bearing itself to the sun and a sunshade covering his eyes. Why can't his father let him do what he wants? His brother is allowed to do whatever, but not him. What was he going to do about this situation? He pondered.

He has always loved to paint, but his father won't hear of it, preparing him all through his life for business, to take up the family company. He knew no matter how much he ran from it;

he would still take up the position of the CEO and he would be able to handle it well, but what happens to his painting? Maybe he can still do it alongside run the company. He needed time, time to be responsible, time to make a good decision, time to wrap his head over all these thoughts. All these thoughts running through his head paused as he saw the striking beauty blond walk up to one of the chairs close to the pool.

Anytime, he sees her, his hands were always itching to paint. She was a jaw-dropping beauty, of course he has seen beautiful ladies but this one was something and the fact that she doesn't say more than few words intrigued him. Surprisingly, he hasn't said anything to her since they got on the boat, his usual self would have walked up to her, flash his charming grin, say one or two things and have her on his bed like a full naked chicken on Christmas dinner, left to him to do what he wants but he hasn't done any of that and he wondered.

Deciding he still wanted her on his bed, he climbed out of the water, wrapping a towel on his waist and walked up to her.

'Hey beautiful', he grinned looking down at him.

Clara looked up and saw Derrick grinning down at her, she almost rolled out her eyes. What does he want now? She wondered. She has avoided him all through and now he was standing in front of her.

'Hi', she replied flatly.

'Mind if I sit?' He questioned gesturing to the reclining lounge chair beside her.

She shrugged, 'do as you please', she said not caring if he sat or not. She was putting on a bikini, with a towel around her shoulder and a shade covering her eyes. She came out to swim and enjoy the serenity of the deck, when she noticed someone was in the pool, so she decided to sit out and wait till the person came out, if she had known that person was Derrick, she would have gone back to her cabin. Now she's stuck.

'Why didn't you come into the water, you obviously came to swim?' He asked as he signaled to the steward who just walked by to get them a drink. When she saw what he was doing, she reacted, 'I don't need a drink'.

'Oh, you will be needing it soon if not now', he spoke out, gesturing to the scorching sun with a smile. She looked up and silently agreed with him but didn't say anything.

'You haven't answered me', he said.

She looked at him, knowing what he meant but didn't want to talk, 'what?' she asked with a frown

'Why didn't you come into the water', he repeated?

'Because I didn't want to?' she replied with questioning eyes, like what is your problem dude?

'That's not true', he said wanting to get to her.

'And how would you know that?' She retorted, now pissed.

'You wouldn't come here putting on your bikini, with a towel on your shoulder, if you didn't want to swim, you are smarter than that', he said looking at her with a smirk on his face.

She wanted to wipe that smirk off his face with a slap, why would he sit there and act like he knows everything, she asked herself.

'Look, Mr. Derrick, I don't know why you are in my business but I need you to get out of it now'. She told him in a raised up and pissed off tone.

'Take off your shades', he said instead. She whirled her head to him, she was fuming now, the courage he has! He was just full of arrogance, she thought, she was about to tell him off with a piece of her mind when the steward arrived with their drinks and left in a hurry sensing the tension around them. Derrick turned away from her, removed his shades and smiled secretly knowing he has gotten to her.

'You know, every time I see you, my hand itches to paint. I have always loved to paint right from the moment I could hold a brush and recognize a picture. My mum was a very talented artist before she died, she was very good, she could paint anything and anyone, she taught I and my younger brother how to paint, but when she died, my father erased every trace of painting in the house, moved us to London and banned us from painting.

He did everything within his power to make sure I and my brother learnt everything about business just to take up the family company later on. The pressure is more on me than my brother, in fact he is allowed to do what he wants but I am not. I really want to paint, but my father wants a different thing from me, he is on my neck and I can't breathe. That's why I came here to clear my head and make a decision'. He narrated with a longing in his eyes.

Once Clara noticed he was sharing something deep about himself, she pulled off her shades, relaxed back and listened. 'I am sorry about your mother, what happened to her?', she asked softly with emotions, feeling like she knew what he was going through.

'She died of cancer, she died when I was 15', he whispered, he still feels the pain of losing his mother at a very young age till date. She gasp lightly, almost stretching out her hand to him to comfort him, she thought otherwise instead, she said, 'I am sorry Derrick, but why did you tell me all these?'

He took a gulp of the fruit juice beside him, stood up and smiled, not looking like someone who just shared his story with a total stranger, 'because I wanted to', he said and walked away leaving Clara discombobulated and annoyed.

Who was this man? Clara questioned herself, with her mouth hanging open as she watched him walk away. She shook her head, stood up and dived into the pool, she would think of what just happened later, for now, she would enjoy her swim, she concluded.

Philip woke up with a splitting headache, it took him a while to remember where he was, when he did, a flash of the night before made him jolt out of the bed.

'I have messed up badly', he groaned while he rubbed his hands over his face. He stood up went to the bathroom to freshen up, once he was back to the room, he called the kitchen in the yacht through the intercom, telling them he wasn't coming out for breakfast, instead they should bring it up to his room with some aspirins for headache , all the while praying they won't send Avery up here.

Now he was in the room, standing and looking out of his room through the window of the cabin. He hasn't gone out since morning and was planning to tell them to bring up his dinner again, he was avoiding Avery, he almost kissed her last night.

'What the hell was I thinking?' He questioned himself as he slammed his fist on the wall.

She helped clean up his mess three times, first the glass, his cuts and the stain of blood on the floor and instead of thanking her, he wanted to kiss her? Wait, she said something about taking his sadness away, right? He couldn't remember exactly what she said, but he knew he almost blurted out his heart to her last night. Maybe he needed her, maybe she would be the one to eventually take away these pains, this loneliness or maybe not. Would she would use him like Leticia? He asked himself all these questions and became more confuse.

As he pondered over these thoughts while staring out of the window, something caught his attention, it was the sound of a beautiful low laugh, he searched with his eyes to get the location of the sound and when he found it, he couldn't breathe, right before his eyes was the most beautiful and warmest smile he has ever seen on a person's face.

Avery was standing with another steward and laughing at whatever the steward was saying, the look on her face was so breathtaking that he ran to get his camera and took a shot, saving it for his eyes only. The way she looked up to the guy, made his throat tightened and he felt like punching him. Who was this guy to her that she was smiling so lovingly at him? He questioned with a frown on his face.

'You were rejecting her help yesterday and now you are getting jealous over her today, get a grip of yourself boy', he told himself, while he walked away from the window.

It has been five days now since she has seen Derrick, after that stunt he pulled back at the swimming pool and she found out that she actually wanted to see him and talk with him.

Clara was sitting at the lounge, sipping a cocktail, she had her hair made today and visited the spa, she felt quite contented, she has been herself here more than she has been in years. She smiled more often and was happy, she has even become freer with Philip, and she kept smiling, as the memories of their constant joking and teasing at each other whenever they were together flashed at her.

She thought back to the conversation she had with Derrick days ago and she couldn't still wrap her heads around it. She used to think he was a spoilt and arrogant man, not until that afternoon, did she realize something, Derrick had issues too. Funny, she feels like telling him of her problems too

She has always kept everything in, not having friends or anyone to share her worries to, she hasn't actually felt like sharing to anyone until that afternoon. It was like Derrick was talking about her but in another version, she likes her job though but she didn't like being controlled by her mother. For the first time, she wanted to talk to someone, even though he was a stranger, but the spoilt brat didn't even give her the opportunity to say anything before he walked away.

'Someone is looking extra beautiful today', she heard a voice say, putting a hold on her thoughts, she looked up to see a smiling Coy and gave him a smile in return. Coy has been really nice to her since she came, always asking of her well being , making her feel things her mother never made her feel.

'Well, thank you, it is the courtesy of the beauty salon here', she said grinning. Her blond hair was straightened and styled up, making her look like a doll.

'They did a good job then', he said while he sat down across her.

'How are you?' He inquired.

'I am fine, I feel elated today', she squealed.

He laughed, the way her face lights up every time he asked her how she was doing made him wonder and happy at the same time. He wondered what her story was, he knew there was an underlying story there, but until she was comfortable to share, he wouldn't ask, he was just happy making her smile, she was like a daughter he never had.

'Can I ask a question?' Clara asked.

'Sure', he replied.

'Why are you always nice to me, even when I am cold?' She questioned.

He was taken aback, not a question he was expecting, he sat up, took one of her hand in his and smiled, 'Because you are beautiful and strong, you might have a lot of things going on with you, but you still stand up strong against the world, I see the inner you and I know you have a lot of things to offer the world. So even when you are cold Clara, I know that's not who you want to be, you want to be that lady that lightens up the world and you just need a little loving to discover that. Your father and mother are lucky to have you. You can have what you want, don't let anyone make you think otherwise, and Clara, I would love to see that smile of yours always', he finally said.

Her eyes were stung. She was trying so hard not cry. How can a stranger say the very words she has always wanted to hear from her mother? She thought. These were the kindest words she has heard and right there, she knew she had great respect for this man and she wouldn't want their friendship to end in that yacht, after all, he could be the father she never had.

'Thank you Coy', she said with a big smile. She knew she could conquer the world at that minute, thinking about Derrick, she felt she could share this found happiness with him since they were almost in the same world.

Chapter 10 – Game and Spa

Staying in the yacht, exploring and acquainting himself with interesting and famous people have been exhilarating but things weren't getting better with him and Alice. Alice has been so cold to him since their first night here. At least, the argument was there before, but now, it was just silence, cold deafening silence between them. That first night of the dinner, he knew something was wrong with her, he tried asking her when they got back to their cabin but she kept saying, 'it is nothing' and it infuriated him beyond words. He slept that night angry and confused.

'What did he do wrong? Weren't they supposed to work things

out together?

All these thoughts went through Jeffery's mind as he sat down at the lounge with the men watching a football match. Every man in the yacht, except the captain and engineer were sitting in the lounge watching football, it was EURO2020, and Switzerland was playing against Russia. The women went together to the spa on Alice invitation, saying they needed to bond too, since the men were already bonding over a football match.

The problem now is that Jeffery wasn't concentrating on the match. Alice was the center of thoughts running through his mind. She wouldn't say more than few words to him, even when she needed his help with something in the room, she would rather try to do it herself or call the attention of a steward and sometimes he sees it and helps her without her asking. Hell, the space between them on bed was bigger than it used to be, this is one month now since they embarked on this trip and he was suffocating from the heightened tension. It wasn't like the tension wasn't there before they came on board, but work helped him think less about it and most times when he comes back home, he made sure Alice was asleep before he goes up to bed. Now there was no work, he wasn't avoiding her, she wasn't talking to him and his balls were getting bluer by the day. Damn! He needs to do something fast or he would be bending any other lady over and fucking her till she could no longer walk very soon.

The shouts of triumph pulled him out of his faze, looking up to the screen to see Russia scoring a goal against Switzerland. He was in support of Switzerland, so the current result of the match soured his mood further.

'Hey man, why the sour look?' Coy asked him with a nudge on his arms.

He couldn't just blurt out to him that his marriage was a mess, so he said instead, 'The match isn't going in my favor man', sighing convincingly, only that Coy wasn't convinced.

Clapping his back slightly, Coy said, 'The match hasn't ended, but then I would vouch for Russia, and I won't be able to wipe your tears away'. He gave a mocking laugh making Jeffery's face look at him with a confused face.

'I thought you wanted to console me man', Jeffery said, while shaking his head with a smile and pulling back his attention to the screen.

Coy looked at him, he knew Jeffery wasn't a happy man. He had sensed the tension between him and Alice right from the first dinner everyone had together and he was sure they came on this trip solely because of the marriage. Coy knew if they left here like that, their marriage would be heading to the gutters, having experienced this before.

He shook his head as he thought, 'poor Jeff, he probably doesn't know what do to fix all of this'.

Nudging Jeffery again, Coy said, 'I can see it in your eyes man, you are not happy and it is not because of this match'. He said, catching Jeffery's attention.

'You love her, but it isn't working out. Have you tried tracing the root of the problem? When you newly got married, were they things you were doing that you are not doing now? When was the last time you took her out? When was the last time you made her know how beautiful she is? When was the last time you asked her about work? When was the last time you both sat down to cracked jokes and talk about random things? When was the last time you told her anything about work?' He continued.

Jeffery stared at Coy, he doesn't know how this man knows he isn't happy with his life but then the questions he was asking him were questions he couldn't reply positively to. He sighed and looked up at Coy.

'What do I do now?' He spoke softly, in a defeated tone.

'Fix it man. The arguments are not there because you guys disagree with everything, it is there because the both of you have given space for a rift to come in. Maybe you used to be her best friend before you got married and now you aren't even close to being friends. Let her know you see her Jeff, let her know you care, and then you would see how open she would become to you. You have to fix it'. He said finally.

Jeffery knew Coy was right. After the 3 years of their marriage, he had a hitch in business, his ex-financial administrator mismanaged the funds of the firm and tempered with a client's case, putting the reputation of the firm at risk. Throughout that year, Jeffery was more in the office than in the house. He was trying to build back every reputation and money he lost that he forgot he had a home, it was after that his marriage started crumbling. Business became fine, but his wife was constantly getting at him and he was irritated he didn't even try to find out what the problem was till it escalated to the point they were almost breaking apart. He shook his head while he thought about all Coy said.

Looking back at the man, he said, 'thank you Coy, I would fix it'. Coy nodded and smiled, 'You do that man. Now let us watch how Russia carries the victory home', he said, gesturing to the screen, while grinning, glad he was there to intervene, before their case becomes like his.

'The hell, they won't!' Jeffery replied feeling better than he had in years, knowing he could still fix his falling marriage. He definitely made the right decision of coming here, he thought as he looked around and saw Derrick arguing with a steward who wasn't buying the idea that Russia was going to win the match, 'at least he wasn't alone' he felt, smiling at the steward.

Alice was happy she didn't go to the spa alone, if not she wouldn't have found a way to escape her thoughts, even though currently she was finding it difficult to push them away. She is not a happy woman; her marriage would fall anytime soon and she felt like a failure. She hasn't been talking to Jeffery since their first night in the yacht, because there was nothing to say.

She came to a conclusion that Jeffery doesn't love her or find her attractive anymore and maybe she irritates him, that's he finds a way to always disagree with everything she says or do. She hasn't spoken about anything to him since that night because she was afraid she was right about Jeff not finding her attractive anymore.

Now she was in the spa with the ladies and she would enjoy herself without any interference of her thoughts, she thought to herself as she tried to push them faraway, which was proving very difficult.

'How long have you been working here, Avery?' Alice asked Avery, as they sat in the sauna with their hair wrapped up in a towel and another on their body. Alice had insisted that every stewardess come with her to the spa since they were not doing anything serious and the boys were busy watching the match. Currently they were in the sauna steaming up.

Avery was in different world of her own, that was why she didn't hear Alice's question. She was thinking about Philip at the same time about the life she wanted for herself. She felt alive thinking about Philip, she had always been that kind and good girl everyone thinks didn't have needs. Always wanted a deep and contented love in her life, a happy ending kind of love. All she wanted was the man of her dreams, have beautiful kids with a lovely home everyone envies and be that woman that can help anybody in needs. She didn't grow up with a silver spoon in her mouth, so she knew what it meant to be hungry and homeless.

'Avery?' Alice questioned in a louder voice causing Avery to pull out of her thoughts.

Startled, she looked towards the direction of Alice, 'sorry, were you talking to me?'

Alice smiled knowingly seeing her dreamy eyes, 'Oh you were daydreaming and yes I was talking to you'.

'Oh, I am sorry, what did you say?' Avery asked.

'How long have you worked here?' Alice repeated.

'I have been working here in Atlantic yacht for 4 years now. I was a waitress at a bar in Mexico when I saw the vacancy on the paper, and I decided to apply and was accepted immediately and here I am now', she replied with a smile, not knowing why she said all of that, but it's been so long since she sat with people and just have meaningful discussions, in fact this is the first time since she started working on the yacht that the guests would sit with them and act like they are people of the same caliber.

'We were accepted the same day', Emily chipped smiling.

'Oh, that's good', Alice said.

'How do you cope with not seeing your family for months?' Clara asked, directing her gaze to Avery.

'It wasn't easy, but I was already used to it. My parents separated when I was in high school, their separation was difficult for everyone to handle, at a time everyone got used to it, with me going away to college and just keeping in touch with them over the phone, there wasn't really anything like family. So coming down here, without seeing them for months, it wasn't really hard. Though I visit them, once in a while, like during Christmas', she replied.

She hasn't really told anyone about this, so she felt a little funny telling it to people she didn't really know, but what is the harm in it? She thought.

'Oh', was the only thing Clara replied

'Oh, poor Avery, you didn't tell me and you made me rattle every time to you about my family', Jersey said dramatically. Avery just smiled at her.

'I am so sorry to hear that Avery', Alice replied. 'Do you know why they separated?' Alice asked Avery.

Shaking her head, she replied, 'I don't really know the genesis of their problem, but after their separation, my mum kept saying she wished she was more open in her marriage, she wished she didn't assume and kept quiet when things were happening to them. She always said to me, 'Avery, never you allow a problem linger in your marriage, once you sense a problem no matter how little, speak out and settle it, it is your responsibility to do so, don't leave it till it keeps accumulating, it would break you' Her words that constantly ring in my head are 'Love your partner without restrictions, love isn't everything, but love conquers all'.

'These words I won't forget, when I find that special somebody', Emily remarked.

'Wow', Alice replied to what Avery said as she fell back to her thoughts. Has she been the cause of the turmoil in her marriage all this while? There have been problems a long while, but why did they let it linger? Has she been keeping quiet instead of talking? Can she still fix it? She loves Jeffery no matter what goes on between them and she would try to fix this. All these Alice thought as the conversation moved from serious topics to random matters.

Chapter 11 - Makeups

Jeffery walked back to their cabin only to see Alice lying down with her back to him. After the match, he wanted to rush back to check if Alice was in so they would talk and settle their issue once and for all, but Coy stopped him and persuaded him to have one or two drinks with the men to celebrate their victory. Even though he wasn't exactly happy with the fact Switzerland the lost match, he still decided to stay and drink and think about the strategy to use in winning back his girl.

Now here he was staring at her back, not knowing what to do. Was she sleeping? He asked himself as he dragged his gaze from her and climbed into the bed. What was he going to say? Where would he start from? He thought boring his eyes into her back. With determination, he raised his hands and placed it softly on her arm.

'Al, are you awake?' He asked softly.

She heard him entered the room. She was nervous, she didn't know what to say, she had carefully arranged her speech, but once she heard him enter the room, everything she prepared went flying out of her head. Maybe they won't be able to settle this, she thought giving up as she pretended, she was asleep, not until she felt the dip of the bed and his hands on her arm did a little spark of hope creep in.

'No', she replied softly.

'Al, can you face me? We need to talk'. He continued. She turned to face him without letting out a word.

When she faced him and he looked at her with her hair packed up and her face devoid of any makeup, a flash of their memories together years back flashed at him and right then and there, he knew that nothing would take his girl from him, they belonged to each other forever. He sat up on the bed, resting his back against the bed and pulling the covers up to his torso.

'These past few years, haven't been easy. I have not been the best of husbands and I am really sorry. I see you Al, and I know you are not happy. Please talk to me, I am here, I am not going anywhere. What do I do that you don't like?' He asked her, all the while looking at her with a broken expression.

What she saw on his face broke her heart. She got up and imitated his sitting position. Sighing, she said, 'I haven't been the best of wives either and I am sorry. But Jeff, you don't see me anymore, you don't even know what is going on in my life, we hardly talk about anything, you no longer compliment me and it makes me wonder if you really still love me, if I irritate you or if you are no longer attracted to me'.

'Wow! He exhaled. 'I don't love you? I don't find you attractive? Babe I am fucking hot for you every damn time, maybe I don't show it every time, but hell, why won't I be attracted to you?' He sighed. 'But why didn't you tell me all this while?'

She wrung her hands together, looking down at them, 'Baby you remember that time your firm was going through some crisis? You hardly saw me, I thought you needed space to clear the mishap and balance yourself, so I didn't say anything. I tried supporting the little way I can, but it wasn't even visible to you at all, you weren't really coming home, you hardly ate at home, we hardly talk about the progress of the firm. Anytime I asked you, you would say, 'it is coming up, don't worry yourself', you pushed me away Jeff. So many things went through my head that period, was I not enough? Am I not a good wife? Have I done anything wrong? I couldn't tell you, I felt it would be selfish and inconsiderate to complain about anything when you were going through so much. That was when it started Jeff, I started feeling less than enough'. She concluded.

He stood up, not able to take what he was feeling any longer. How could he be so selfish? How he didn't figure out all this while, he thought as paced the room. Turning back to Alice, he saw the tears fall off her eye, she is a very strong woman and hardly cries so when he saw them roll out, it broke his heart.

'Al', he said as he climbed back into the bed, kneeling facing her, 'I am so sorry, I was the selfish and inconsiderate one here. I was supposed to talk about my problems and progress with you, but instead, I tried solving everything by myself pushing you out, thinking I was trying to save you some stress. I didn't want you worrying about anything, I didn't know not telling you will make you worry. You are enough for me, you are everything I want , everything I need, I love you so much and I would never again in my life let you feel less of yourself'. He said, almost close to tears.

She was sobbing now, she knew there was love between them, but she just realized they didn't love themselves the way they should have, loving themselves with everything, without doubts and assumptions.

'I was always mad at myself for not talking and at you for not seeing me, that was why any opportunity I saw to make an argument I took it, just to let out my anger', she said as she sniffed.

'Come here', was all he said, as he gathered her up in his arms. She held his body and cried harder, they've wasted so many years, just because they were just assuming and not talking. She raised her head and look up at him to ask him one question that has been buried deep inside of her.

'Jeff, don't you want to have a baby with me?' He paused and looked at her, what the hell has he done? He questioned himself.

'Why would you say that, Al?' He asked, gently pushing her back a little to see her properly.

Sniffing, she said, 'because, you've never talked about us trying, which made me feel you think I am not enough to carry your baby'.

'Wow, wow, wow, hold it up there Al, you were the one who said you weren't ready for a baby when we got married, that was why we got you on those birth pills. I thought when you were ready you would let me know. I want a baby with you sweetheart, a little girl with your eyes and smile and a boy with your strength'. He said, raising her chin with his hands and looking so lovingly at her.

'I really thought you didn't see me capable enough to carry your child, that was why you didn't argue with me from the beginning or say something later on', she said while looking up at him.

'You know what baby, can we just stop thinking and start making babies now?' He said with a grin as he gently pushed her against the mattress and stayed on top of her, supporting himself with his arms.

'Really?' She giggled as her eyes descended on his lips.

Seeing her smiling like that, he didn't know he was able to survive not being with her all this while, it was unexplainable, maybe he had super powers to resist beautiful women, he thought.

'Gosh Al, I have missed you so much', he huskily said as he pressed his lips against hers, loosing himself in the euphoria of her lips.

Alice moaned into his mouth, her hands running through his hair, she felt contented, she knew she could conquer the world at this point. It was her and Jeff against the world, she won't make those mistakes again, rather she would learn from it. Before she knew what was going on, her clothes and that of Jeffery's were a pile on the floor, he was rough and impatient and so she was. They would take what they want this time, next time they can be gentle, she thought as she wrapped her legs around him, titling her wet core invitingly to his cock.

He teased her with his tongues swirling round her nipples and his fingers stroking her core, 'Jeff, now please, I can't wait again', she said as she moaned out loud and writhed under his arms.

'Wait, I have been meaning to ask, why were you so cranky at that first dinner party we had here, it was more than me not pulling out the chair right?' He asked. 'You didn't tell me how I looked; I was…ah… eager…oh my… to hear from youuuuu!!' she stuttered with a scream when he added a second finger to the one already deep into her core.

'I am sorry baby', he said as he positioned himself at her entrance, ready to drive her insane, he moved back to her lips, kissing her like his life depended on it, he paused, looked up at her, 'How many babies do you want my darling?' he asked, grinning like he just won an award when he saw her struggling to breathe.

'Oh my God, Jeff, you can give me as many babies as you want to, just FUCK ME!!! She screamed, not minding if anyone was hearing her. He laughed and whispered, 'I love you Al' as he entered her with so much force, making them groan out loudly. She wanted to tell him how much she loves him, she wanted to remind him they haven't had dinner yet, but no words could take form in her mouth, so she stopped struggling to talk and enjoyed the love ride. They both found a steady rhythm and rode themselves into euphoria bliss.

The yacht docked at Ho Coc Beach in Vietnam. Some of the crew members went to a nearby village in Vietnam to get a refill of groceries and some equipment needed on the yacht and the engineers did some servicing on the yacht's engine. They were very close to Palawan Islands and everyone was excited as they were all eager to explore.

Ho Coc beach has a primitive but wonderful five kilometer stretch of golden sand; the beach has clear waters and it is very good for swimming. There is a Binh Chau Hot spring that is conveniently kept nearby, incase sunbathing gets too much and seafood restaurants around at its far end. They would be staying there for a few days before they continue trip.

Philip stepped out the yacht to get a good sight of the beach. He has been enjoying this trip so far but still felt empty and he had a feeling, Avery could help him out. He walked around the beach, he was barefoot, wearing with a short-sleeved shirt with 3 buttons popped up, a short with a very dark sunglass. You could see a glimpse of his muscular chest through the open buttons, his hair was wavering with the breeze as he walked with his hands in the pocket of his short.

He wasn't going to go back to Toronto like this, he thought, he had to do something and the only thing he could think of was letting out what he felt to someone, maybe he would feel better. Apart from his best friend, Sandro, no one else knew what exactly happened between him and Leticia, even his best friend didn't know the extent Leticia actions cut into him. He was too ashamed to tell anyone. Now this Avery girl had a way of making him blurt out something he couldn't say to his best friend, he was going to talk to her, if it is going to make him feel better, he would tell her of his pains and let her soothe him, or he would just talk and leave, that is it, that is what he will do even though it sounded stupid, even to his own ears, he concluded as he went back to the yacht in search of her.

Avery was on the lower deck in the yacht narrating to Stefano of her encounter when she went to get groceries with the chef. Over the years, she and Stefano have become friends. She could sit with him all day and gist. He was very friendly and has smart mouth that throws witty comments making you laugh or leaving you annoyed. Even though she doesn't share deep things with him, she still enjoys their conversations and his friendship.

Currently she was telling him of how the chef got mesmerized by the woman behind the counter where they went to get stuffs and how she had a hard time pulling him out of there. They were both laughing and were so caught up in their gist that they didn't notice the figure standing behind them until she felt the hairs at the back of her neck standing, she turned, her smile altered and she froze immediately she saw the person standing behind her.

Philip was fuming as he watched her laugh with the same guy he saw her with days ago, who is this guy to her? He questioned within himself. But the moment she turned to look at him, his world stilled. He wanted to hug her at that moment, nothing mattered then than just staring at her. Her brown hair were let down to her shoulders in big curls, her face was plain, apart from the mascara on her eyes and the pink gloss that coated her lips and he wanted nothing better than to feel those lips against his. What will it feel to kiss those lips? What will it feel to hold her against his body?

He was back to reality from those thoughts by the clearing of a throat, he blinked and looked around to see the steward guy looking between him and Avery, he looked back to Avery to see her looking anywhere but him.

'Can I have a word with you?' He said to Avery needing to break the tension around them.

She blinked at him, he wants to talk to her? She was puzzled.

Taking her hesitation as denial, he added, 'Please?'

Avery, realizing he was serious, nodded at him and looked up to Stefano and said, 'give me a minute Stefano, I would be right back'.

'It would be more than a minute', Philip said as he looked at Stefano, eyeing him and acting like he wanted to punch him.

They stood there for a while in an eye battle only breaking it when Avery said, 'Okay, Philip lets go', while she looked at Stefano with pleading eyes.

Philip nodded to her and walked her to the sky lounge at the upper deck. 'Please have a sit', he said, as he pulled out a chair for her. Instead of sitting, she was staring at him with her hands folded under her arms with a questioningly look. Realizing she wasn't going to sit.

He sighed, 'what is it?'

'Firstly, what was that thing you did down there? And secondly, why did you bring me up here to sit and have a word?' She stressed on 'word', getting pissed.

'I don't know the answer to your first question and you would only get the answers to the second if you would just sit down and let me talk', he said while resting his hands on the chair he pulled out for her. 'Please', he added.

Looking at him, she decided she really wanted to know why he wanted to talk with her, so she sat with a huff, 'Okay fine'.

Philip didn't know if he was making the right decision, he was nervous as hell but he never backed down on any decision he makes. He sat down on a chair across from hers. 'Should I get you a drink?'

'Look, Philip just talk, I have some other things to do', she said impatiently, she wanted him to get to the point, not because she was in a hurry to back to her duty but because she was very curious. What does he want to say? She questioned herself.

'Okay, so I can't really remember the exact words you said to me the other night, but I know you said, you wanted to take away my sadness, you wanted to make me feel better. Did you mean it?' He asked peering down at her.

She was panicking. Did he remember? Why did I even tell him? How am I going to explain myself? Yes, I meant it but what is he going to do knowing I meant those words I said? Should I say no? What if he thinks I was playing with his feelings? No, I can't lie. Calm down Avery, calm down, she told herself.

He saw the look in her face and knew she was probably afraid of the inevitable if she answered the question. He wanted her to know he wasn't going to hold anything against her, he just wanted to know the truth.

'Look Avery, I know it is somehow to say those of words to someone you don't really know, but most times, the heart knows what it wants, even before you do. It is important I know if you meant those words. Did you mean it Avery? Do you want to take my sadness away?' He asked in a soft voice.

She heaved out a sigh from her lips, 'Yes Philip, I meant every of those words I said that night. I could see the sadness in your eyes, and I just wanted to take them away and make you feel better'.

It was like she was picking up the shreds of his heart and placing them together one by one when she said those to him. He felt peace.

'I used to have a girlfriend; her name was Leticia. We were together for 3 years before we broke up. She broke up with me actually, and I was never the same after then. I really loved her, that I could do anything and everything for her. She loved money, lots of money, wanting to get the new bags, clothes or shoes in town. I wasn't bothered because I could afford it. I thought she loved me, she would fight any lady who came an inch to me, and held me possessively like I was a damn prize. I thought it was love, I didn't know I was just a prey she had caught and decided to keep for herself. Everything was going fine until I started noticing how obsessed she became about money. Frequently, I would see huge transactions made by her from my account. It began affecting me financially. I couldn't complain because I was afraid she would get angry and leave, I even had plans to marry her', he said as he shook his head.

'My money was dropping deeper and deeper and I didn't know what to do. One day I tried questioning her about it, she got angry and busted in tears, asking me why I would question her about what she does with the money, that I am making her feel she is mismanaging the money and she is a good for nothing. I don't know how she came up with that conclusion, but I just apologized and let it go not until this faithful day. I was at work when I got a message, a message showing the debit of almost all the money in my account. I was dumb founded, I ran out of the studio and drove like crazy to the house, only for me to hear grunt and moans. My girlfriend was with another man in bed. I caught them pants down'. He breathed out. 'Do you know the painful part?' He asked visibly shaking making Avery stretch out her hands to hold his. Once she held his hand, he grabbed it tight.

'I was so mad, confused, distraught and hurt. The only thing I could say was why, the only thing I could ask was why, and the bitch laughed and told me in these exact words, 'I have waited a long time for this, I have gotten what I want and I would be leaving with the love of my life right here on this bed. Thank you for the life you gave me Philip, I hope you find someone for yourself'

I didn't know what to feel or think, I walked out of my own house, feeling the weight of my stupidity. Everything was right before me, but I didn't want to see it. I felt like I had lost everything, I couldn't even tell my best friend what had happened'. He finally said with a tear rolling down his eyes.

Avery's heart was shattered. How can someone be so mean? She thought. How someone do this to a gentle loving man like this? She thought as she forced herself not to cry. If she could get her hands on that Leticia girl, she would tear her to pieces. 'I am so sorry Philip; you don't deserve all that. Do you still love her?' Avery asked.

Shaking his head, 'I used to ask myself, which one was more painful, losing her or losing all my money on a gold digger, but over time I realized losing her was the best thing for me and when I came to that realization, everything I felt for her died. So no, I don't love her anymore'. He replied.

Avery nodded and held his hands tighter and looked at him, feeling a pull at her heart, he has gone through so much, someone with so much love inside of him doesn't deserve a woman like that, she thought.

'The first time I saw you Avery, I wanted to share my pains with you. I felt you could bring me back into the world I lost and when you said those words to me I knew I had to follow my instinct. I don't know what this is, I don't know why my heart feels the way it feels, but Avery will you help me love again?' He asked as he held her hands tight and looked longingly into her eyes.

She looked at him and her eyes welled up. Right there she knew this man held her heart, there was no turning back for her. Philip felt his feet back to earth as she nodded and pulled him into the most peaceful hug he has ever had.

Chapter 12 – The Reveal

It has been 2 weeks, since they had their adventure on Ho Coc Beach. Things between Jeffery and Alice have been very good. They haven't had one argument since their makeup night and the love making was limitless, even though Alice acted like they should slow down a bit, she was secretly enjoying the attention Jeffery was giving to her. It was like they were newly married; the joy and happiness were overwhelming. Jeffery was ready to do anything to make her extra comfortable. They explored the yacht together, from the swimming pool, to the lounges, the cinema, to the sauna, and down to the luxurious bathroom in their cabin. Alice thought she couldn't be happier.

Today, the captain announced their arrival on the Palawan Islands and everyone was excited beyond words. They would be spending some time on the Island before they head back to their different locations. The opportunities for adventure on the Island are endless. It has some of the most exciting and challenging dive sites in the world with a myriad of marine life to view and photograph.

Now they were on the Island and Philip felt more alive than he has felt in a long while. Things between him and Avery have intensified, they were seeing each other every day while they are on the yacht. Sharing things about each other, he learnt about her challenges while growing, the fact she came from a poor background and the separation of her parents. He realized she was that girl posed like she was worry free, but in fact has so many worries of her own. It was through one of their discussions, he knew she studied her business in college and has always wanted to own her own bar, that was why she worked as a waitress in so many bars before she came to work in the yacht. When he asked her why she applied for the job on the yacht, she said, she needed the money to open her own bar. He smiled then and secretly promised himself that he would make sure she owned that bar.

Avery was a strong lady and the more time he spent with her, the more he realized what he has been missing all his life. He doesn't understand all these new feelings he had for her but he was eager to explore, he was tired of wallowing in heartbreak, he needed a breath of fresh air and Avery was that breath of fresh air, he needed Avery. He was thinking about all of these and taking pictures of the majestic mountains and shimmering beaches on the Island, when he heard, 'Hi, Phil'.

Turning to the cheerful sound, he saw the smile of the woman that takes his breath every time, he couldn't resist her beautiful smile, he took up his camera and quickly took a picture.

'Really?' she said laughing with her head thrown to the back. Grinning, Philip took another picture of her, he kept on clicking on the camera until he was satisfied.

'That's enough', she said smiling as she wrapped her arms around him. She was in love with this man, she probably was the first day she looked into his eyes, they haven't exchanged any declaration of love yet, but she knew he felt something for her.

Looking up at him she asked, 'how are you today?'

'I am better now that I am seeing you', he said beaming down at her as he wrapped his arms around her. He was just few inches taller than she was.

She giggled, 'Oh really?'

'What? You don't believe me?' he asked with an expression of tenderness. 'Avery I don't know what you did to me, I know you did, but you've made me see brighter than I have in years, you've given me a reason to look forward to the next day. You brighten my day, Avery. So, I meant it when I said I feel better when I see you', He said finally.

She was contented, she knew she had what she always wanted in her arms, the man of her dreams. She had never experienced love, always wanting but never having it. He was right, the heart always knows what he wants, even when the head doesn't, she thought as she looked deep into his eyes, 'I love you Philip Langley', she said quietly.

Those words did something to his heart, he didn't know if what he felt was really love. He was a man that has been in love before but what he knows was different. He couldn't say those words she wanted to hear now, he couldn't say them until, he was sure. But one thing he knew was, he didn't want her to leave him and he did just that thing his heart was tugging at him to do. He kissed her.

The butterflies in her stomach were numerous, her legs were getting weaker, her world was spinning and her heart was beating so fast in her ears. It was gentle, slow and soul capturing. The kiss didn't make her run away, it made her want to stay in his arms forever. There and then, Avery knew she would never regret this decision as she held on tighter to him for dear life.

Derrick wasn't as disturbed as he was before he came on this trip. Now he was on Palawan Island and all he could think of was what he was going to do when he gets back home. Will he take up the business? Will he do it alongside painting? Would he just forget about the company and pursue his painting dreams? All these thoughts ran through his head as he stands by the beach, crossed legs, playing with the white sand.

He looked up and saw Clara walking up to him, he smiled. Ever since their encounter at the pool, they've always found ways to talk to each other. He knew he wanted her in his bed, but she was different, he couldn't have her like other girls. He found out he was freer to talk with her than he had with any other person. They had almost the same story and it is refreshing to know that someone understood his stand.

'Hi', she said as got to him and bent down to imitate his position.

'Hi yourself', he replied, turning to look the running waters.

'What are you doing here all by yourself?' She asked, looking at him.

'Thinking', he shrugged, still not looking at her.

'Oh', she replied quietly with a nod.

'People used to think I am an arrogant, spoilt and irresponsible rich kid. Sometimes I agree with them though. The thing is, everything I have secretly always wanted, I never had. My dad had a way shaping my life in to what he wants, not what I want. I found a way to transfer those desires into arrogance. I took any woman I wanted, anything money could buy, I took it without thinking twice, I tried hard to be irresponsible, so my father would leave me alone, but it only become worst, now I feel so very less of myself.' He said after 5 minutes of silence between them.

Clara looked at him, 'Derrick, you are a wonderful person. I don't really know so much and the little I know, I discovered how bold you can be, how gentle you are on the inside, and your sense of humor is something I admire. You can't compare yourself to anybody. You are amazing just the way you are. You can be who you want to be, you can decide to run the company or become a very famous talented artist, or you can have the both. Anyone you choose Derrick, you would be known for someone who influences humanity and the world would see how great of a person you are', she said.

Derrick was looking at her now, those words she released from her mouth might be mere words to anybody, but to him, they meant a lot. 'I think I like you', he said grinning at her.

'I don't like you though', she said trying not to laugh.

'Really?' He asked as he turned his body to her.

'Really', she said with a straight face, finding it very difficult not to laugh.

He reached out to her and began tickling her. 'Are you sure?' he asked her.

She broke out into fits of laughter, 'Derrick, wh…attt….are …y...ouuu doing?!!!' She screamed as she struggled to get up.

He stood up pulling her with him, the moment she got to her feet, she picked up her sandals and raced past him, laughing so hard she couldn't breathe well, Derrick chased after her and it was not up to a few seconds before he caught up with her, pulling her arm, they both landed on the sand with her back against the sand and him on top.

'You still don't like me?' He asked with his brows raised and a grin on his face.

She gave him a heart stopping warm smile, 'I like you too', she said knowing she has a found a friend in Derrick, she doesn't know what the future holds for them, but she would definitely open up to this new found friendship.

Since they got to the Island, Alice hasn't been feeling too well, she has been feeling weak and tired frequently and has lost appetite. She didn't want to tell Jeffery, since she thought it was just change of environment, but this morning as she sat looking at breakfast, she couldn't stop the nauseous feeling that was welling up inside of her. She just sat and stared at the food trying so hard not to throw up as everyone was at the table the men mantled that morning for breakfast, close the beach.

'Babe, what is it? Why aren't you eating? Jeffery asked her in a hushed tone.

'I don't feel good Jeff', she replied with a grimace.

'What is it? Is it your head, your stomach?' He asked looking worried. Before she could say anything, she stood up and ran far away from the table to throw up. Jeffery ran after her, he got her and held up her hair so the vomit won't touch her hair.

Emily saw what was happening and ran to them, 'is everything okay?' She asked when she got to them.

'Alice doesn't feel good, she didn't even take anything before she threw up', Jeffery informed Emily.

The moment Alice raised her head and looked at her, she knew what the problem was. 'Jeffery why not you go back to breakfast, I will take up from here', Emily said.

'Are you sure?' he asked Emily with questions in his eyes. 'Al?' He directed his gaze to Alice silently asking if she was okay with it.

'Jeff, I am fine, just listen to Emily and go back to the table, I would eat later'. He nodded still not sure of the decision, he walked back to the table.

The moment he got to the table, everyone asked him questions, he just told them she would be fine as he wondered what could be wrong with his wife.

Emily led Alice back to the yacht, to the medical room. On their way to the medicals, Emily blurted out, 'you are pregnant'.

'WHAT?! Alice shrieked. 'How do you know that?' Alice asked her feeling apprehensive now.

'My mum used to be a matron before she retired, and I have had many experiences with pregnant women before I started working at the yacht. But let's get you tested, I might be wrong', she said as they walked into the room and requested for a pregnancy kit.

Few minutes later, Alice came out to meet Emily outside the medical room with a terrified expression, 'I am pregnant', she whispered.

'Congratulations Alice', She beamed with a smile but frowned when she saw the expression on Alice face, 'this is good news right?' She asked

'I don't know what if I am not a good mother? I didn't know it would happen so soon. I didn't take my pills recently but I didn't know.......' she trailed off as Emily held her in a bid embrace.

'I have seen you Al, you would be a great mother and I am sure this baby cannot wait to be in your arms', Emily said soothingly, she understood what was happening to Alice, she has seen it so many times, the uncertainty of a mother.

'Thank you', Alice whispered as felt a little better, the only thing that would make her feel better than she felt currently was her husband, she taught as she gently pushed herself from Emily. 'I need to tell Jeffery', she said.

'Yeah, sure go ahead, I bet he would be so happy to hear the news', Emily said as she let her arms fall to her sides and nudged Alice forward.

'Thank you, Emily', Alice said to her with a sweet smile as she embarked on the journey to meet the newest father in town.

She was nervous, as she got closer to the table she noticed, they were done with breakfast and were just having a conversation. The moment Jeffery saw her, he stood and ran close to her.

'Sweetheart, are you okay? Are you fine? Did you go to the medicals? Did they say anything? What took you so long? 'He filled her ears with questions. He held her, while he bent down to look into her eyes, waiting for answers.

'Jeff, I am pregnant', she whispered.

'Excuse me, what did you just say?' He whispered back.

'I am carrying your baby Jeff, you are going to be a father', she told him as she gently rubbed her stomach.

He stared at her fazed. 'I am going to be a father?' He asked. Still whispering, when she nodded smiling up at him, He shouted, 'I am going to be a father!' lifting her up and spinning her around.

She laughed out with her heart full of joy, 'Jeff let me down, I feel dizzy' she whined.

'Sorry my love', he said as he dropped her on her feet and ran to rest on the table. 'I am going to be a father!' he announced, pumping his fist into the air. Congratulations were in the air;

everyone was happy for them.

Alice walked slowly to the table to receive their kisses and hugs. She was so grateful she agreed to come on this trip. She had her husband back, her happiness, her joy and a beautiful baby on the way. She wouldn't trade this happiness for anything in the world.

Avery stood at beach, peering at the sky, the stars were shinning bright and the moon was full. She stood there thinking about her life, about her parents, her work and Philip. She knew she wanted to have a life with Philip outside there, because to her, life on a yacht wasn't the real world. She didn't know his plans, she didn't know if she was in his plans, she didn't even know if he loves her, she feels he does but she needs to hear it. The breeze blew, carrying her hair up with it, loving the feeling of the breeze on her skin, she whirl around.

Philip laughed as he watched her, causing her to stop so abruptly, she almost tripped. He has been looking for her all around only to find her here all by herself. Today they explored Palawan together. He had to take permission on her behalf from the yacht's manger just for them to have their time alone. He was happier than when he came and smiled more often.

'You scared me', she said with a pout.

'Sorry darling, I didn't mean to, you just looked like a child when you rolled like that', he said as he drew closer to her. 'What are you doing here by this time, all by yourself?'

She shrugged, 'thinking'.

'Am I in those thoughts?' He asked smirking.

'Maybe, maybe not', she replied, snickering.

'I love it when you do that', he said, curving her face in his palms.

'Do what?' She questioned.

'When you smile like that'. He replied, his eyes boring into hers, she doesn't have an idea how much she turns him on with her small gestures, he wanted to see the sparkle in her eyes when he pleasures her, he wanted to hear moan out his name, he wanted her to hold unto to him for dear life, when he enters her, he thought as he tried to control himself, he was hot for her.

Avery could feel the tension, her heart was beating so loud she was afraid he would hear it. The way he was staring at her, made her wet in between her legs. She didn't know how someone could affect her way Philip did. She was waiting for his next step when she heard him whisper, 'I brought something for you'.

Philip knew that was not the place or time to have those elicit thought, so he musters up every strength he had to remember what he was looking for and why he was there.

'What is it?' she whispered back. He dropped down his hands and reached for the bag across his shoulders and opened it, before he brought out what was in it he said, 'close your eyes'.

'Phil, seriously?' She whined.

'Yes baby, close your eyes', he said. She looked at him, nodded and did what he told her.

It wasn't up 2 minutes when he said, 'you can open those beautiful eyes now'.

She did as she was told and gasp out loudly with her hand covering her mouth and her eyes widened, before her was a beautiful framed picture of her laughing with her head thrown back and a total sense of happiness written all over her face, in Philip's hands. She stretched out her hands to collect the frame and caressed it with her fingertips. Nobody has given her a gift before, except her parents on Christmas. She could remember when Philip took this picture, he was able to capture something she hadn't seen in herself for a long time. Happiness, she was happy, Philip made her happy, maybe Philip could finally give her the happy ending she has always wanted.

'You like it?' he asked beaming.

'I love it Phil', she said as she threw herself into his arms. He hugged her tight, the joy on her face was enough for him.

She disentangled herself from his arms and looked up at him, 'but how did you do it?'

'That's my secret baby'. He said ginning like a Cheshire cat.

She just stares deep into his eyes, wanting him to just know she meant the words she was about to say to him and said, 'Thank you so much Phil, thank you coming into my life, thank you for giving meaning into my life. I love you'.

He was happy she was happy, he liked making her smile, he like seeing her eyes glitter when she smiled. She came into his world and made it blossom with happiness. He wasn't that glooming Philip anymore, he had something to look forward to every day, which was making his Avery smile and, in that moment, he knew that in all his 28 years, he was never sure of something as he was at that very minute. He loves her, plain and simple, he loves Avery.

'I love you Avery', he said, not waiting to get a response from her, he pulled her gently to him and claimed his prize, and when she moaned into his mouth, he knew Sandro made the best decision for him.

We are at the end, if you enjoyed this trip like I had the pleasure to write it, please let me know your thoughts with a review on amazon.

Thank you! It will be a pleasure to have you also for my next books.

https://www.amazon.com/review/create-review

Lightning Source UK Ltd.
Milton Keynes UK
UKHW020347100821
388593UK00002B/392